Severed Bloodline

Copyright © 2023 Ron Chapman

All rights reserved

No part of this publication may be reproduced or transmitted in any form or by any means, electronic or mechanical, including photocopying, recording on any information storage and retrieval system without the written permission of the author except for the use of brief quotations in a book review.

This book is a work of fiction. Names, characters, places and incidents are products of the author's twisted and disturbed imagination. Any resemblance to actual persons living or dead, events or locations is purely coincidental.

Edited by: Ron Chapman

Cover artist: Ryan Chapman

Cover model: Tabitha Wininger

Beta readers: Heidi, Sibbie and Tabatha

Kringle
Severed Bloodline

**By
Ron Chapman**

My inspiration for writing are my three wonderful children and a comment made by my youngest, "Daddy, why don't you quit your job so you can spend more time with me."

The inspiration for the stories that I write?... LIFE.

Santa's study is as it was since his death, dark, quiet and for the most part, undisturbed and unchanged. It's as if Santa's study were frozen in time.

Santa's study is neatly cluttered with artifacts from around the world from all his travels. There's floor to ceiling book shelves jam packed with hundreds of old books, some of which are priceless and out of print. Pictures of Santa and Holly are hung all over the study. Some of the pictures are of Santa and Holly when they were kids while others are of them as they celebrated their time together throughout the years. There's even a picture of Santa and Holly when they were little and sitting on the laps of Santa's mother and father. Little gifts that children from around the world made and left for Santa on Christmas Eve are scattered about Santa's study, gifts that Santa didn't have the heart to throw away and that are now collecting layers of dust.

Nowadays, it's just Holly that uses her husband's study and even then, she just sits back in her husband's chair and stares off into space thinking about all the times her and her husband shared together.

On occasion, when Holly isn't staring off into space, she'll start a fire in the fireplace and tinker around with some of her husband's old toys.

Tonight…

A white taper candle is burning away on Santa's desk as an old and neglected jack-in-the-box gets a new lease on life with a few brush strokes of a paint brush.

The old rust on the jack-in-the-box's metal box has been sanded away and repainted with a snowy winter wonderland scene, complete with Santa being pulled in his sleigh by his eight reindeer. There's also silver and gold trim all around the jack-in-the-box.

Holly puts her paint brush down and sits back in the chair her husband has used so many times.

As Holly admires her handy work, "There you go my friend, as good as new. And ready to go to a new home, if such a one still exists."

Table of Contents

PROLOGUE   1

ONE
The Sickness   4

TWO
The Beginning of the End   10

THREE
A Second Chance at Life   15

FOUR
Coach Stall's Emasculation   22

FIVE
Chocolatey Goodness   36

SIX
The Harvest   44

SEVEN
Father Murphy's Twisted Confession   47

EIGHT
Whack-A-Mole   57

NINE
Choke N' Stroke   68

TEN
Double Vision   79

ELEVEN
Mommy's Here to Save The Day   87

TWELVE
Trailer Park Trash   106

THIRTEEN
A True Apex Predator   112

FOURTEEN
Last of The Pups   129

FIFTEEN
Daddy Dearest   146

SIXTEEN
Severed Bloodline   158

SEVENTEEN
Death of an Alpha   168

EIGHTEEN
Arctic Enema   185

NINETEEN
Mounting The Holiday Herd   194

TWENTY
The Final Goodbye   200

EPILOGUE   203

BONUS MATERIAL   207

In Colonial America, a lit candle was placed in a window so that it would light the way for a safe return for weary travelers of family members.

PROLOGUE

The stories of Santa and who he is have been told to children for centuries and passed down through generations of families. Stories of a round jolly old man with a white beard and wearing a red velvet coat, pants and a hat with white fur trim as he is being pulled around in a sleigh by eight reindeer; Dasher, Dancer, Prancer, Vixen, Comet, Cupid, Donner and Blitzen.

The stories also tell of Santa touching the side of his nose and magically disappearing down chimneys with a huge red velvet bag full of gifts for all the nice boys and girls. And for those children who are naughty and not so nice, they are not left out. They too get a gift. It may not be the gift they wanted but they get a gift in the form of a few lumps of coal in their stockings.

It is these stories that have made Santa a holiday legend. Some may even say an immortal.

But if Santa is truly immortal like the stories have made him out to be, then some of you might be wondering...

Why did Santa die and disappear when he was shot by seven-year-old Napoleon in Kringle, A Twisted Christmas Tale? And why did all the elves and most of the holiday legends die as a result of Santa's death?

Here is my explanation.

Santa exists in the minds and hearts of the children who have not yet grown up and still believe in the stories told to them about Santa.

But with each passing year, there are fewer and fewer children not believing in the holiday legend known as Santa, making him just as weak and susceptible to sicknesses and injury as a mortal man his age would be.

Santa is only as strong as the number of children who believe in him.

So, when seven-year-old Napoleon looked into the scope of his gun and saw what he saw, Napoleon chose not to believe and instead, chose to pull the trigger.

Because of the actions of a seven-year-old boy, Santa and the magic of Christmas ceased to exist. Both of which became nothing more than a distant memory in the minds and hearts of the children throughout the world.

Without Santa around to protect the elves and the other holiday legends with his magic, the elves and a handful of the holiday legends died as a result of a young child who no longer believed.

Something else you might be wondering about is, if Santa, the elves and the holiday legends died, how was Holly and a handful of the remaining holiday legends able to survive?

Well… Here is how that happened.

Because of the time spent with Santa's family when she was younger and then later as Santa's wife, a small amount of Christmas magic rubbed off onto Holly but not nearly as much as Santa had. Holly only had enough Christmas magic to keep a few of the remaining holiday legends and family members alive. Because she only had a limited amount of Christmas magic, Holly was forced to pick and choose who shale live and who shale die.

So, other than that, Holly has no real magical ties with Santa. The only attachment she has with Santa is strictly emotional, heart and soul.

Holly was born with magical powers of her own, some of which allows her to control the winter elements, which would explain how she was able to manipulate the weather in Kringle, A Twisted Christmas Tale.

In the end, the death of Santa, Holly's husband, her only one true love gave birth to a whole new holiday legend, one that will not soon be forgotten.

1

THE SICKNESS

When someone dies, you have got to dispose of the body whether it's six feet under or in some kind of mausoleum. Some people even cremate their dead.
Long ago, such a place was created for the citizens of Christmas Village. How and when it happened is unknown.
If you are lucky enough to somehow find the location of Christmas Village and fly over it, you'll see just a little over a hundred yards behind the main living quarters is an enormous trench maze in the shape of a snowflake with two eight-foot-tall nutcrackers guarding the entrance and many more nutcrackers throughout the interior of the trench maze that are elaborately decorated in Christmas colors.
In the middle of that snowflake, you will also see a huge mausoleum with two more eight foot all nutcrackers guarding the entrance of the mausoleum as well.
The two nutcrackers guarding the entrance of the mausoleum are decorated in silver and gold.
The trench maze was meant to be used for the citizens of Christmas Village and the mausoleum was for the Kringle family and close friends.
The thing is though, the citizens of Christmas

Village have a long-life span so, the number of citizens buried in the trench maze and in the mausoleum can be counted on two hands. And until recently, the trench maze was empty, leaving only Kris Kringle's parents, grandparents from both sides of his family and the remains of Holly's mother and father in the mausoleum.

That is until Kris was killed. Then all hell broke loose.

With the death of Santa Claus and no successor to carry on the Christmas spirit, the Christmas spirit slowly faded away from Christmas Village.

Christmas Village was changed forever.

Caroling and the Christmas cheer stopped. There was only sadness and despair.

Everyone in Christmas Village became withdrawn from everyone in the village and isolated themselves to their living quarters.

Since Eggnog, Prancer and Vixen did not seem to be really affected by the sickness that was wiping out the other citizens of Christmas Village, Holly used whatever Christmas magic she had gotten from her husband to keep them from getting sick and even then, it took everything she had. And since Holly was not a true holiday legend, there was only so much she could do with what she had.

Having the power to control the winter elements was not much use for those sick and dying.

Since Frostbite was born in the Himalayan mountains and was not a true holiday legend like everyone else in Christmas Village, he too wasn't affected like everyone else.

Oh sure, Christmas Village had an infirmary, but it was set up to treat minor cuts and scrapes, maybe a broken bone here and there and an occasional birth. Christmas Village's infirmary was never meant to handle the decimation of Christmas Village's population.

Holly did not even have time to mourn the loss of her beloved husband or the death of the six reindeer she helped raise and train since they were calves.

The first of three muffled church bells, the passing bell echoes throughout Christmas Village.

In the beginning stages of the sickness, it was just a couple of Christmas Village's citizens that got sick. Then after a few days, the sickness spread throughout Christmas Village like wildfire.

The citizens of Christmas Village got so sick that they began to die, left and right. It got to be where there were three to four deaths a day, sometimes more. The citizens of Christmas Village were dying faster than they could be buried.

There are bodies lying all over the infirmary, both sick and dead.

An old, timeworn Holly is running about the infirmary, doing everything she can to ease the pain of the sick and dying.

A few of the sick elves are lying in the infirmary beds with such bad coughs that they are turning red in the face as they cough up blood.

One of the sick elves clutches onto Holly's dress as she walks by.

Holly stops and turns around.

The elf that grabs Holly's dress is Bell, one of Holly's oldest and dearest friends in Christmas Village.

When Holly was brought back to Christmas Village after her parents were killed, with the exception of the Kringle family, Bell was the first to take Holly's hand and make her feel safe in a strange new home.

It might have happened long ago, but Holly

remembers it as clear as day.

Once the sleigh comes to a stop in the barn, the portly, jolly old man helps Holly off the sleigh.
Holly timidly takes in the sights of her new surroundings.
Holly sees several stalls with reindeer in them. Some of the reindeer are sleeping while others are eating.
Holly's eyes well up as she starts to miss her mother and father.
A three foot tall woman with pointed ears and long flowing blond hair walks up to the sleigh with a big warm smile.
Two, three foot tall men with pointed ears unharness the reindeer from the sleigh.
One of the pointed eared men leads the reindeer off to a stall while the other pointed eared man puts away the harnesses.
"Hello Santa." The three foot tall woman greets Santa with a big warm smile.
"Hello Bell. Would you be so kind as to take our new friend and find her some dry clothes?" Santa asks.
"Sure." Bell extends a hand out to Holly with a smile and waits for her to take it.
As Santa steps off his sleigh, "Go on, she won't bite." Santa looks at a scared and wet Holly but then motions to Bell.
Bell introduces herself to Holly. "Hi, my name is Bell. Come on, we'll get you out of those wet clothes."
"Oh, and Bell..." Says as he takes his wife's hand.
Bell stops and turns around while still holding Holly's hand. "Yes Santa." She responds.
"When you're done seeing after Holly, would you please find Kris and tell him that his mother and father would like to speak to him?" Santa asks Bell.

"Yes Santa." Bell kindly answers Santa then continues walking out of the barn with Holly.

Holly looks back at Santa and his wife who in now at Santa's side.

Santa and his wife watch as Holly is taken to get a change of dry clothes.

Present time.

Bell's hand trembles as she holds onto Holly's dress. "P-p-please mother. H-h-help me."

Holly pulls up a stool and sits beside her dying friend.

Holly can remember a time when Bell's eyes were big, bright and twinkled with excitement. Now Bell's eyes are sunken into her pale, bony face. Her once long flowing blond hair has fallen out.

Holly knows there is nothing she can do for her tiny, frail friend but lay a loving hand on her cheek and try to smile through her sadness.

Now it is Holly's turn to take her friend's hand and make her feel safe as she goes off to a strange new home.

In the back of the infirmary, Vixen rushes to her friend's side and gently wipes the blood from the side of his mouth while putting a cold rag on his head to try and bring his temperature down.

A second muffled church bell, the death knell echoes throughout Christmas Village.

Elsewhere in Christmas Village, Prancer has been tasked to go door to door and paint a big red cross on the doors of those that are already dead or too far gone for any kind of help.

Back in the day before the sickness, all the buildings had their front doors decorated with holly and wreaths instead of a big red cross.

Prancer sniffles as she moves on to the next-door with her can of red paint and paintbrush. She passes Frostbite along the way.

Frostbite is pulling a large wooden cart behind him that he's using to transport the dead to the trench maze. The cart is loaded down with the bodies of Frostbite's dead friends.

Deep in the trench maze, Eggnog is dressed in his finest monk's robe.

He is standing in front of nine headstones that have been recently recessed into the side of the trench maze.

The headstones belong to Eggnog's wife, daughter, his infant son, mother, father and his two sets of grandparents.

Eggnog is crying hysterically at the loss of his whole family. He drops to his knees and continues to cry in his hands.

A final muffled church bell, the lynch bell echoes once more.

2

THE BEGINNING OF THE END

Many years later.
A younger Holly, the twins, Frostbite, Eggnog and Mr. Heat are standing upwind of a slight cold wintery breeze.
Holly's head and face are hidden by a hood. She is also wearing a red velvet dress with white embroidery along the hemline. She is also wearing a full-length cloak that is made of crushed red velvet and trimmed out in white fur around the collar, cuffs, hemline and along the front. A black leather belt with an antique gold buckle is keeping Holly's cloak closed around her waist. Holly's capelet and hood are also made of crushed red velvet with white fur around the edges. Her capelet is drawn closed with a white cord that has a white pom-pom on either end of the cord.
Holly is also wearing white satin gloves and black leather, Victorian boots that go to just below her knees and lace all the way up.
Vixen and Prancer are both wearing matching Eskimo styled, stretched crushed brown velvet skirts that stop a few inches below their crotch. Each skirt has an oversized hood with pom-pom ties.
The hood, cuffs and hemline are trimmed in white fur.

White mittens cover their hands.

Vixen and Prancer are also wearing white boots that stop below their knees and lace all the way up with brown laces. The boots are also trimmed in white fur.

Eggnog in his best monk's robe and Frostbite are standing behind Holly while Mr. Heat and his black and white pinstriped suite are standing beside the twins.

Mr. Heat licks his lips as he eyes Prancer up and down.

Prancer notices Mr. Heat's hungry eyes and shoots him a disgusted look then quickly turns away.

All six of them are standing quietly behind a forty-foot-tall white cedar tree, watching as a funeral is taking place.

A short, stout, sixty-year-old priest with a graying horseshoe haircut is delivering a homily as a fairly large group of people, including children, are gathered around three headstones.

The priest holds his hands up to the sky for a second or two then brings them together in front of him. "Thank you Lord for giving us Napoleon, Caroline and Mandy.

Thank you Lord for letting them come into our lives and filling our hearts with so much love and happiness.

Now we ask you to please give us the strength to move forward as we give them back to you, with the knowledge that they will be living on forever as they look down on us from the heavens above.

Through Jesus Crist.

Amen"

As the people that are gathered around keep their heads down, they all respond with, "Amen." Some of the people are even crying.

As the priest continues his good word of the Lord, a little boy catches a whiff of pine and cinnamon. But as the winter breeze continues to blow, the little boy smells what he thinks is a skunk. The boy lifts his head up and smells. There is also a slight odor of dead fish in the air.

The little boy quickly covers his nose and mouth with his hand.

Prancer and Vixen take a step closer towards the funeral.

Holly gently puts a hand on Prancer's shoulder to stop them from going any further.

The twins turn and look back at Holly.

Holly pulls her hood off. "No. Let them mourn the loss of their loved ones. When they are finished then we will sever their bloodline and make them pay for what they've done."

Frostbite grunts while barring his teeth.

The twins shapeshift into their reindeer form.

The little boy's eyes are red and swollen from crying. He sniffles then wipes his runny nose on his sleeve. The boy then turns around just enough to see behind him and when he does, off in the distance, the little boy sees a woman dressed in what looks to be a red female version of a Santa suite, two white reindeer, a giant furry monster, and a short man wearing a brown monk's robe with one of his hands on one of the reindeer.

The little boy also sees another man with bright, fiery red hair and dressed in a black and white pinstriped suite. This man is slightly taller than the man in the monk's robe and he is standing next to the other reindeer.

In this time of sadness, the little boy manages a little smile as he notices the strange people and monster watching him and his family.

Holly takes a step back and as she does, a small snow devil rises up from the snow-covered ground and circles Holly's feet. The snow devil is growing in size as it travels up Holly's body.

Once the snow devil has completely enveloped

Holly, it is well over six feet tall and eight feet in diameter. Frostbite and Eggnog turn and disappear into the swirling snow devil.

Vixen and Prancer are next to walk into the snow devil but not before Mr. Heat pinches Prancer's reindeer ass.

Prancer quickly shapeshifts into her human form and reaches back around to slap Mr. Heat's face. "You fucking pig!" Prancer then disappears into the snow devil just like the rest of her family did.

Mr. Heat smiles as gets one foot into the snow devil while rubbing the side of his face where Prancer slapped him. He is stopped from going any further when he is pushed away from the snow devil by a hand coming back out of the snow devil.

Holly steps out of the snow devil. Her face is hard and rigid. She quickly grabs onto one of Mr. Heat's ears and yanks up on it so hard that Mr. Heat is forced to stand on his tippy toes.

Mr. Heat winces in pain.

Holly sticks one of her fingers in Mr. Heat's face and verbally assaults him. "I'm only going to tell you this once so listen up. I will have your head ripped off your pitiful body and piss down your neck if you ever touch one of my family members again. UNDERSTAND!"

The little boy's mother bends down to her son's ear and gently pulls back on his arm to turn him around. She whispers in his ear. "Turn around and pay attention."

"But mom." The little boy protests as he turns around again and points to where the strangers were.

The boy's mother looks to where her son was pointing but she doesn't see anyone.

Holly and her family have disappeared.

"Turn around." The little boy's mother whispers again.

The little boy disappointingly does as he is told and turns back around.

3

A SECOND CHANCE AT LIFE

A pack of hungry gray wolves, eleven total, stalk their prey in the snow covered evergreen and spruce trees surrounding lake Inari, Finland.

It's been a long frigid winter and it's been even longer since the wolves have last eaten. But tonight, they will feast. The wolves will feast until their bellies are engorged.

A reindeer drawn sleigh is carrying Igor, Lavia and their eight-year-old daughter, Holly, down a snow-covered path, unaware they are being hunted by a pack of hungry wolves.

Igor, Lavia and Holly are enjoying the winter sleigh ride along lake Inari.

Holly rests her head on her father's arm.

Igor and Lavia glance at each other with warm, loving smiles. They then look down at their daughter who is taking in her winter surroundings with such delight.

Holly notices that her mother and father are smiling at her. She returns their loving smiles and then takes her arms out from under her warm blanket. Holly takes one of her mother's hands and interlocks their fingers.

Since Holly's father is holding onto the reins with both hands, Holly wraps her free arm around his arm and rests her head on his arm that she is holding.

The smile on Holly's face is so big that it stretches from one side of her face to the other as she enjoys the sleigh ride with her mother and father.

Holly couldn't feel any safer and loved than she does now, nestled between her mother and father.

Igor notices the woods have become eerily quiet.

As the reindeer pulls the sleigh down the snow-covered path, a small winter breeze blows across Igor's face. He smells a musky odor in the air. It is then that Igor realizes that he and his family are in danger.

A horrific look washes over Igor's face as he quickly looks around.

Lavia sees the look on her husband's face. "What is it dear?" She asks in a concerned voice.

Igor grips the reins even tighter. He quickly looks at Lavia just long enough to say, "Hang onto Holly."

Lavia quickly pulls Holly close to her and holds onto her as tight as she can.

With a couple flicks of the reins, the reindeer starts to run as fast as it can.

"Mom, what's wrong?" Holly asks as she wonders why her mother has drawn her closer to her.

Lavia ignores her daughter's question but then with a terrified look on her face, Lavia asks Igor the same question. "Honey, what's wrong?"

Igor doesn't answer Lavia instead, he flicks the reindeer's reins, pushing the reindeer to run even faster.

The sleigh carrying Igor and his family violently bounces up and down as it hits a hard snow mound on the path while being pulled by the reindeer.

It's only seconds after asking Igor what was wrong that the answer to Lavia's question makes itself known.

A pack of hungry wolves leap from the shadows to chase down Igor and his family.

Lavia screams as she holds onto Holly with her dear life. "IGOR!" Lavia points to three wolves running up onto Igor's left side of the sleigh.

Two more wolves are running along Lavia's side of the sleigh. One of the two wolves leaps at Lavia.

Without thinking, Lavia extends one of her hands towards the wolf that is leaping at her. Hundreds of small quills made out of ice shoot out from the palm of Lavia's hand and hits the wolf that's leaping at her.

The wolf yelps then drops into a snowbank along the snow-covered trail. The wolf rolls around for a bit then jumps to its feet and continues to chase after the sleigh

Another wolf leaps off a large boulder and lands on the back of the reindeer pulling the sleigh.

Holly hollers to her mother while pointing at the wolf on the back of the reindeer. "MOM!"

The reindeer lets out a loud groaning sound as the wolf sinks its teeth into the back of the reindeer's neck.

Igor struggles to keep control of the sleigh and reindeer.

The reindeer turns abruptly onto a frozen lake Inari. "DAD!" Holly now screams for her father.

The wolf on the reindeer's back, rips out huge chunks of the reindeer's neck.

Lavia shoots more ice quills at the wolf on the reindeer's back but as soon as the reindeer steps onto the frozen lake, the reindeer loses its footing and falls as it slides across the frozen lake, taking the sleigh with it.

The sleigh tips over on its side with Igor, Lavia and Holly still in the sleigh.

Lavia smashes her head on the cold, hard, frozen lake. She lies sprawled out and motionless. Blood from a huge gash on Lavia's forehead is staining the ice and snow around her head.

Holly rolls out and away from the turned over

sleigh. She is crying as she lies on her side.
Igor is lying across Lavia's back. He moans in pain as he tries to get to his hands and feet.

The reindeer is struggling to stand up, but three more wolves savagely attack the reindeer, knocking the reindeer backdown to the frozen lake. The wolves tare chunks out of the reindeer and eat it.

With rosy, red cheeks and tears streaming down her cheeks, Holly watches as the reindeer that was pulling her family's sleigh is being eaten alive by the pack of wolves.

Holly can hear the flesh of the reindeer being torn away from its body.

Holly then notices more wolves surrounding either side of the tipped sleigh, three on one side and two on the other side of the sleigh.

The wolves crouch, ready to pounce as they slowly make their way towards Holly. Their ears are erect. Their fur is bristly and standing upright. The wolves' lips are curled up, displaying their sharp incisors as they snarl.

The wolves are so focused on Holly, they don't see Igor or Lavia.

Holly gets to her feet and reaches for her father. She then hollers for him. "DADDY!"

Igor sees the wolves that are within inches from his little girl. He quickly takes a deep breath and exhales, blowing out towards Holly.

A chilly winter breeze blows Holly further out onto the frozen lake and away from the wolves.

Holly falls to her hands and knees as she is blown out of harm's way.

"DADDY! HELP ME!" Holly hollers for her father again.

The wolves take off running after Holly.

Holly comes to a stop. She is crying hysterically.

The wolves are almost upon her.

Igor touches a bare hand to the frozen lake. Seconds later, ice rises up and around Holly, forming a thick protective ice dome around her.

Because the wolves are running full speed on the frozen lake, they are unbale to stop when the ice dome forms around Holly so, they run right into the ice dome.

A couple of the wolves yelp when they hit the ice dome.

Two more wolves jump on the tipped-over sleigh. They look down at Igor and Lavia. Both the wolves are crouched backwards, ready to pounce on Igor and Lavia.

Igor is so worried about his daughter's safety that he is unaware of the two wolves above him until it's too late.

Inside the safety of the ice dome that her father has put around her, Holly is crying for her mother and father. "Daddy… Mommy…" Holly hugs her knees into her chest. She is terrified.

All Holy can hear from inside the ice dome are the wolves clawing and scratching to get in.

When neither of her parents come to get her, Holly eventually cries herself to sleep only to be awaked sometime later, still inside the ice dome that her father put around her and lying in a puddle of water. She is soak and wet.

Holly's eyes are bloodshot and swollen from crying. Her cheeks are red and blotchy.

Holly rubs her eyes then looks around the ice dome, wondering why her mother or father hadn't gotten her yet. She listens for the wolves, but she cannot hear them. Still, Holly is afraid to say anything for fear the wolves might still be waiting for her.

It's got to be early morning because Holly can see light shining through the ice dome around her.

A shadowy image is also seen slowly walking

around the ice dome.
　　　The ice dome is slowly melting in the early morning sun. Water droplets from the melting ice is dripping on Holly like a steady rain shower.
　　　Holly watches the shadow slowly move around her protective ice dome.
　　　The shadow stops. It reaches for the top of the dome and gently raps on the top of the dome.
　　　Holly backs up.
　　　A small hole opens up in the top of the ice dome.
　　　A wrinkled old woman wearing gold rectangular framed glasses peers in through the hole. The old woman is also wearing a white bonnet with red and white ribbon trim and holly on one side of the bonnet.
　　　Tufts of white, curly hair have escaped from under the woman's bonnet.
　　　The old woman looks down at Holly and with a bit of sadness in her voice, "Oh dear."

　　　Present day – early morning
　　　Holly stands with her hands in her pockets, on the edge of a frozen lake Inari with snow covered evergreens and spruce trees behind her.
　　　Holly is looking out onto the frozen lake thinking, until she hears some tree branches cracking and breaking behind her. She can also hear the snow crunch under foot as someone approaches.
　　　Holly breathes in the frigid winter air. She smiles as she realizes who is coming.
　　　Frostbite breaks more trees as he walks up behind Holly.
　　　Holly looks up at Frostbite with a smile. "There's no sneaking up on me, my old friend."
　　　Frostbite grunts, almost as if he were disappointed that he was discovered.

Holly looks back out onto the lake. Her smile disappears. "Do you know I almost died out there when I was just a little child." Holly pauses then, "Then I was given a second chance at life only to have that one taken from me as well."

Frostbite shifts his weight in the snow.

"It's time to take back what was taken from me. And believe me... I won't be merciful." Holly looks up at Frostbite. And this time, instead of smiling, she has rage in her eyes.

4

COACH STALL'S EMASCULATION

    It's a sellout game at the Bulldogs' football game, at least it looks like it on the Bulldogs' side of the bleachers. There isn't an empty seat to be found.
    With all the loud cheering, the Bulldogs' sports commentator is barely heard over the loudspeakers. "A light snowfall blankets the Bulldogs' football field as the bulldogs and Panthers take to the field with thirty seconds left on the clock."
    "The Bulldogs trail the Panthers, twelve to thirteen."
    "Both teams line up on the thirty-yard line for the last play of the game… The ball is snapped… Rottson drops back… He's got pressure from the linebacker… The time has expired… Rottson looks to the endzone and let's go of the ball just as he is hit from linebacker, Rigerman."
    "The ball tips the hands of the defender, but Barr snatches it out of the air with one hand. WHAT A CATCH! WHAT A CATCH! THE BULLDOGS WIN! This is one for the ages. I can't believe it. When they talk about Bulldog football years from now, it will be this play they talk about. I CAN'T BELIEVE IT!"
    There's a few seconds of silence then the Bulldogs' sports commentator's voice bellows out of the loudspeakers

once more. "This is Marty Usery signing off. BULLDOGS OUT!"

    An hour has passed since the football game and there is now about a foot of fresh snow on the field. The floodlights that illuminated the football game have been turned off along with all the other lights in the school parking lot.
    The only one left in the school is the Bulldogs' head coach, coach Stall. Everyone else; players, family members, spectators, teachers, and the rest of the coaching staff have all gone home for the night.
    Coach Stall exits the school, surprised at the amount of snow that has come down since going into the school after the game. "HOLY SHIT!" Coach Stall says as he looks around the snow-covered parking lot. He slings his small duffle bag over his shoulder and sighs with a smile.
    There could have been six feet of snow on the ground, and it still wouldn't have mattered. Because of his team winning tonight, coach Stall in on the top of the world.
    Coach Stall turns to lock the door he came out of.
    When the door is locked, coach Stall puts his keys in his pocket but when he turns back around to walk to his car, he is greeted by a blizzard, a total whiteout. The wind has even picked up.
    "What the fuck. Where in the hell did this shit come from?" Coach Stall asks himself.
    The heavy snowfall and fierce winds have created such a whiteout that coach Stall can't see no more than a foot in front of him, if that.
    The whiteout has even swallowed coach Stall's car.
    The wind is blowing in such a way that it sounds like someone is whistling in the whiteout.
    "Fuck, it's going to take me hours to get home in

this shit." Coach Stall thinks for a moment until an idea comes to him. Coach Stall digs in his pants pockets for his keys. "Fuck this shit. I'm going back in and wait this storm out."

Coach Stall pulls out a keychain full of keys and as he turns around to unlock the door he came out of, coach Stall fumbles with the keys until they fall into a snowbank.

"FUCK! GOD DAMN IT!" Coach Stall stomps his foot in the snow then kicks away some of the snow where he thinks he dropped his keys to see if he can find them but, no luck. "Where in the fuck did they go? They dropped right here." Coach Stall kicks around more snow.

Coach Stall can feel the temperature drop as ice crystals start to form under his nose from the snot dripping out.

The snow and wind continue to blow all around coach Stall as he looks for his keys. He can feel the freezing wind blowing through his thick coat and thermals.

Coach Stall struggles to keep his duffle bag slung over his shoulder as he crouches down and uses his hands to move the snow out of the way in hopes that he might find his keys.

As he continues to look for his keys, coach Stall hears a soft-drawn out whistle coming from the direction of the football field or what he thinks is the football field.

"What the fuck. Who the fuck is still here?" Coach Stall stands up and turns around but is unable to see who is whistling because of the snowstorm.

The whistling stops.

Coach Stall is surrounded on all sides by such a thick snowfall that he can't see a thing in front of him, not even the school.

"WHO'S THERE?" Coach Stall hollers to the person who was whistling. Coach Stall quickly turns around, trying to figure out which way is forward.

No one answers.

Coach Stall takes a step into the blizzard but as he does, the blizzard stops abruptly, as if by magic.

Coach Stall looks around and finds that he is standing on the fifty-yard line of the Bulldogs' football field, knee deep in snow.

Coach Stall drops his duffle bag in the snow as he quickly looks around the snow-covered football field. He is bewildered as to how he got onto the football field seeing that he was just by the school.

Coach Stall hears the soft drawn out whistle again. This time, it's coming from directly behind him.

Coach Stall quickly turns around to face the scoreboard at the end of the field, the same direction as to where the whistle is coming from.

A strong gust of wind blows the snow around the football field, creating another whiteout. The blowing snow is making it impossible to see anything.

The snow is hitting coach Stall's face so hard that it's starting to sting.

Coach Stall wipes away the snot icicles from his nose then zips his coat up as far as it will go. He then pulls the hood to his jacket over his head then pulls on the hood's drawstrings until his hood closes in around his face so that just his eyes and the tip of his nose is peering out from the hood.

Coach Stall sniffles as he squints to see who is whistling within the blowing snow. But all coach Stall sees is a wall of snow all around him.

Coach Stall hollers to whoever is whistling. "WHO THE FUCK IS OUT THERE?" Coach Stall waits for an answer.

The whistling stops again. Then the wind and snow stop.

Coach Stall is standing in snow up to his knees as

he looks around the snow-covered football field.

As coach Stall turns to face the scoreboard end of the field, a whirling snow devil rises into the air, ten feet tall and widens to fourteen feet.

Coach Stall falls back onto his ass as he backs up. "What the fuck!"

Holly is the first to step through the snow devil. "Shame on you, Mr. Stall. You've been an awfully bad boy this year."

Holly is wearing a powder blue, velvet Santa dress with her hood over her head.

Coach Stall slowly gets to his feet. "Who the fuck are you, bitch?"

Holly stops. She reaches for the hood covering her head. "I've been called many names in my lifetime." Holly pauses for a brief moment. Then, "But bitch isn't one of them and bitch I am not. You Mr. Stall can call me Holly."

Holly pulls the hood off her head to reveal her blond hair in braids; a tight French braid going down the back of her head with a tight water fall braid on either side of the French braid. Holly also has two French braids on either side of her head, around her temple area.

Holly has an evil looking grin on her face.

While the snow devil continues to spiral around behind Holly, two fully grown, white reindeer cows step out of the snow devil.

As the reindeer walk to either side of Holly, they shapeshift into their human form, Vixen and Prancer.

Once in their human form, the twins are wearing white leather, gothic trench coats.

Coach Stall rubs his eyes. He can't believe what just happened.

Vixen and Prancer put their hands into their coat pockets and look at each other and smile. They both laugh childishly. Then they both look at a surprised coach Stall.

Coach Stall still doesn't believe what just happened. One minute he is exiting the school and the next minute he is on the fifty-yard line of the football field watching a woman step through a whirling column of snow and now two reindeer cows shapeshift into two women who are identical twins.

Coach Stall gathers his courage, puffs his chest out and then takes a step towards the three women. He points a finger at Holly. "I don't know who the fuck you people are but get the hell off my field or I'm going to call the police."

Except for the sound of the wind blowing, there's a few seconds of silence.

Then, Vixen breaks the silence. "You're not going…"

Prancer finishes "…to do anything."

As coach Stall opens his mouth to say something, he smells a skunk then the putrid odor of a rotten fish market slaps him in the face.

Coach Stall gags a few times then doubles over and throws up the greasy hamburger he had after the football game.

Vixen and Prancer giggle.

Holly takes a few steps towards coach Stall. "You've made the naughty list this year Mr. Stall. But don't worry, even the worst of kids get a little surprise."

Coach Stall stands up, wipes the vomit off his mouth and, "FUCK YOU!" Coach Stall gives Holly the middle finger.

Just as coach Stall gives Holly the middle finger, a nine-foot-tall monster covered in fur, muscle and sharp pointed bone protrusions, steps through the snow devil. The monster's hands and chest are stained red with blood.

In the Himalayan Mountains, the monster is a legend that is feared by all, a legend that is known as the Yeti. To his family and friends, the Yeti is known as

Frostbite.

The wind that is blowing the snow devil around also blows some of Frostbite's fur in his face.

Frostbite is carrying a large red velvet sack slung over his shoulder.

The snow devil disappears.

Holly, Vixen and Prancer look over their shoulder at Frostbite.

Coach Stall has both a look of fear and disbelief on his face as he watches Frostbite. Then, "OH SHIT!" Coach Stall quickly turns and runs from Holly and her family.

Frostbite growls at a retreating coach Stall then throws the sack he had slung over his shoulder at coach Stall. The sack hits coach Stall in the back, knocking him face first into the snow.

Holly, Vixen, Prancer, and Frostbite make their way to an unconscious coach Stall who is lying in the snow with a red velvet sack on his back.

Frostbite picks up the sack, opens it and dumps its contents onto an unconscious coach Stall.

Out of the sack falls eight bloody decapitated heads of coach Stall's coaching staff.

A brief time later.

Coach Stall wakes up, on his back, screaming at the top of his lungs as if someone had just stuck him with a hot poker. His eyes bulge as he arches his back. Coach Stall is freezing and shaking uncontrollably. He tries to move his arms and sit up, but he cannot.

Coach Stall's arms are bound behind his back by thick, shackles made of ice. He next, tries to move his legs but they too are immobile.

Coach Stall's arms, upper back and ass are so cold that his skin is pale and numb. Coach Stall also feels a great deal of numbness around his balls.

Coach Stall lifts his head up and notices that he has been stripped of all his clothes and is lying on a large block of ice.

To coach Stall's horror, he sees a guillotine made out of ice in front of him. His legs are bent at the knees with his ankles bound to the sides of the guillotine by the same kind of thick shackles holding his arms.

Coach Stall struggles to see over his round belly.

His pelvic area has been pushed all the way up to the guillotine so that his scrotum and balls are in the guillotine's lunette.

Coach Stall slowly looks up at the blade of the guillotine that's made out of a thin piece of sharpened ice. He panics at the site of the guillotine and struggles to pull away from it.

"WHAT THE FUCK!" Coach Stall screams and thrashes around but it gets him nowhere.

"I wouldn't move around too much if I were you Mr. Stall. That blade looks like it could go anytime now." Holly walks out from behind coach Stall.

Vixen, Prancer, and Frostbite soon follow.

Vixen and Prancer are giggling among themselves.

Frostbite is carrying eight decapitated heads of coach Stall's coaching staff by their hair. When Frostbite steps into coach Stall's line of sight, he throws the eight heads at coach Stall.

A few of the heads roll across coach Stall's naked chest, leaving behind bloody skid marks along his chest. A couple of the heads hit coach Stall on his head then drop into the snow.

With a both angry and horrific look on his face, coach Stall looks at the heads of his coaching staff in the snow. "YOU MOTHERFUCKERS! When I get out of here, I'm going to kill every one of you."

Vixen and Prancer stop their giggling and look at

each other. "Really?" Vixen and Prancer ask at the same time then they look at Frostbite.

Frostbite takes a step towards coach Stall.

Holly gently takes Frostbite's hand and stops him before he does anything to coach Stall.

"No, my friend, this one is mine." Holly tells Frostbite in a calming voice then walks closer to coach Stall. She leans over coach Stall, grabs a hand full of his hair with one hand while firmly grabbing onto his chin with her other hand and forces coach Stall to look at her.

"You my friend, have a big mouth. It's time you shut it." Holly tells coach Stall.

Coach Stall spits in Holly's face. "FUCK YOU BITCH!"

Holly let's go of coach Stall's hair and chin then steps back away from coach Stall.

Vixen, Prancer, and Frostbite all take a quick step towards coach Stall as if they were going to attack him for what he had just did and said to Holly.

Holly puts a hand up to stop her family members as she wipes the spit off her face with her forearm. "I said this one is mine."

Holly walks back to coach Stall. Without saying a word, Holly passes a hand over coach Stall's mouth and as she does, a square patch of ice forms over coach Stall's mouth, preventing him from saying another word.

Coach Stall looks down at his mouth with a look of horror.

The skin around the ice patch covering coach Stall's mouth pulls and stretches as coach Stall tries to open his mouth to scream.

"Now, where were we, Mr. Stall before you rudely interrupted me?" Holly taps her forehead a couple times as if trying to think. Then, "Oh yes, the reason why you are on the naughty list."

Vixen and Prancer flank either side of the guillotine's upright supports as they are now both giggling like two little schoolgirls. Both women look at coach Stall's blue scrotum sack that is stuck in the lunette.

Prancer leans in and swats at coach Stall's cold, blue scrotum sack like a cat would do with a small toy ball. Coach Stall tries to pull away but still cannot.

Frostbite positions himself across from Holly, towering over both Holly, and the terrified coach Stall.

"To hell with teaching the kids the fundamentals of the game. You're the type of coach who likes to win all the time. Aren't you, Mr. Stall?" Holly moves coach Stall's hair out of his eyes. "And I bet you'll even go to any lengths to get that W under your belt, won't you?"

Coach Stall frantically shakes he head back and forth, disagreeing with Holly, while still trying to scream.

The shaking of coach Stall's head is also moving the ice blade of the guillotine ever so slightly.

Prancer stops playing with coach Stall's frozen scrotum.

The twins look up at the ice blade moving with each movement that coach Stall makes. They then look at coach Stall's frozen blue scrotum. Vixen and Prancer then look at each other. Their eyes are big and bright and filled with so much excitement knowing what's about to happen.

Holly puts a hand on coach Stall's head. "Oh, Mr. Stall, I wouldn't move like that again. The release mechanism on this thing is pretty sensitive."

Coach Stall suddenly stops his moving, looks up at Holly then at the guillotine's blade. His eyes are filled with fear as he watches the guillotine's blade move.

Even though coach Stall has stopped shaking his head, his body is still involuntarily shaking from the cold.

Holly leaves coach Stall's side and walks to Vixen. With a slight nod of her head, Holly motions for Vixen to stand by Prancer, leaving Holly to take Vixen's place by the guillotine's upright support.

Vixen and Prancer put an arm around each other and exchange a long sensual kiss with their tongues in each other's mouth.

Frostbite watches the twins kiss for a few minutes then turns his attention back to coach Stall.

Paying the twins no mind, Holly puts a hand on the upright support of the guillotine and continues. "That win is so important to you that instead of giving some of your younger players a shot, you like to stack the team in your favor and call up players from your JV modified team."

Coach Stall shivers from the cold. He turns his head away from Holly.

Holly gently wiggles the guillotine to make the blade move ever so slightly. "Look at me when I'm talking to you, Mr. Stall. I'm not done with you yet."

Holly waits for coach Stall to look at her before continuing.

Coach Stall still refuses to look at Holly.

Frostbite grabs coach Stall's cold and trembling chin with his massive grayish purple hand and jerks coach Stall's head so that he is now looking at Holly.

Coach Stall moans.

Holly slowly but gently closes her fingers around the guillotine's release mechanism.

Coach Stall's eyes widen with fear as he watches Holly's hand grab the guillotine's release mechanism.

"You tell the younger players on your team, they have to earn their spot but yet, you bring in other players who don't earn their spot on the team. Tell me Mr. Stall, how is that fair?" Holly looks at coach Stall and waits for an answer to her question, an answer that is muffled by the ice that is keeping coach Stall's mouth frozen shut. Holly then asks another question. "Do you know that one of your star players, number three, threatened to lay out one of your younger players?"

Coach Stall has a cold, guilty expression on his face.

As if to read coach Stall's mind, "That's what I thought." Holly waves her free hand in front of the guillotine and out of nowhere, the snow devil reappears. She then looks down at coach Stall. "Now we're done."

It takes coach Stall only a second to realize what Holly means when she said, "Now we're done." He screams as loud as the ice covering his mouth will allow him to scream while frantically thrashing around like a wild animal caught in a trap.

Coach Stall's mouth starts to bleed as some of his skin pulls away from the ice around his mouth.

Holly pulls the guillotine's release mechanism then walks off and disappears into the snow devil.

The guillotine's ice blade drops down onto coach Stall's frozen scrotum sack. Like a hot knife through butter, the ice blade severs coach Stall's scrotum sack and its contents from the rest of his body.

The severed scrotum sack and its contents fall into the snow.

Blood gushes out from coach Stall's crotch, staining everything that is touches.

Coach Stall pushes away from the guillotine as much as he can while arching his back in pain. He screams so loud that his lips rip away from the ice patch covering his mouth.

Coach Stall's mouth is bleeding where it ripped away from the ice patch that was covering his mouth.

Vixen and Prancer point at coach Stall's severed scrotum lying in the snow while laughing hysterically. The twins then turn and follow Holly through the snow devil while holding each other's hand.

Because of his thrashing around, the ice shackles holding his arms behind his back break, allowing coach Stall to fall off the block of ice that he was lying on, except for his legs which are still secured to either side of the guillotine.

Coach Stall thrashes around like a fish out of water while screaming in pain.

Blood continues to gush out from where coach Stall's scrotum was severed from his crotch.

Frostbite reaches down and palms coach Stall's face. As Frostbite squeezes coach Stall's face, his sharp fingernails dig into the cold flesh of coach Stall's face.

Coach Stall screams even more as the bones in his face make a cracking sound.

Frostbite lifts coach Stall into the air with his feet still attached to either side of the guillotine.

Coach Stall stops his screaming as his face turns to pulp in Frostbite's hand.

When coach Stall can't be lifted any higher, Frostbite yanks up on coach Stall so hard that the ice shackles securing his ankles to the guillotine shatter. Frostbite then slings coach Stall's lifeless body over his shoulder.

Before he follows his family into the snow devil with coach Stall draped over his shoulder, Frostbite reaches down and picks up coach Stall's bloody scrotum sack, throws it into the air and catches it in his mouth. His jaws snap shut, swallowing the scrotum sack and balls without so much as chewing them.

Frostbite disappears into the snow devil just like his family.

The snow devil swirls around for a few seconds before turning into a light snowfall.

As soon as the snow devil disappears, the guillotine and large block of ice that coach Stall was lying on turns into water where it then mixes in with the snow covering the football field, leaving no trace of it ever being there.

Soon, even the blood-stained snow disappears under a fresh blanket of snow.

5

CHOCOLATY GOODNESS

7:00a.m. Saturday morning.
A loud, irritating buzzing of an alarm clock goes off.
Darnel, an eighteen-year-old, all-star quarter back for his high school football team, the Bulldogs, rolls over in bed. He grabs the irritating alarm clock and throws it across his bedroom where it hits the wall and falls into a waste basket.
Darnel covers back up and goes back to sleep for a few more minutes.
The few more minutes turns into a half hour.
Darnel drags himself out of bed and is now getting ready for football practice.
After taking a shower, Darnel walks down the hallway of his parent's house with just his pajama bottoms on with his muscular torso exposed. He is drying his head off with a towel as he walks downstairs to make himself some breakfast.
Halfway down the stairs, Darnel hears his cell phone ringing in his room. He quickly turns around and heads back upstairs to his room for his phone.
"Hey Chris, what's up?" Darnel talks to his friend while finishing towel drying his hair with his free hand.

"Yea, I'll be at practice. I'm getting ready now."

Halfway down the stairs, Darnel hears his dog barking and takes his phone away from his ear. "WHAT THE HELL ARE YOU BARKING AT, TYSON!" Darnel hollers to his little Shih Tzu.

When Darnel reaches the back door, his dog is jumping and barking at the door to go out.

"The damn dog has a doggie door but he's afraid to use it." Darnel tells his friend on the other end of the phone as he opens the back door for his dog to go out.

Darnel's dog continues its barking as it takes off running out the back door and into the backyard that's covered in a light blanket of snow.

Darnel closes the back door and watches his dog from one of the kitchen windows, racing around the backyard.

Tyson chases a black tan rabbit out of hiding. The rabbit runs for its life, trying to keep away from the little dog.

As Darnel watches the chase taking place in his backyard, "Yea, the party is still on for tonight." Darnel pauses for a moment then continues talking to his friend. "Don't worry. My parents are gone for the whole week. We can party all weekend." Darnel walks away from the kitchen window to get himself a bowl and spoon. Darnel then sits down at the kitchen table. "Alright man, I'll see you at practice then." Darnel hangs up his phone and sets it on the table by his bowl and spoon. He then gets up and grabs a box of cereal out of the pantry.

Darnel walks to the refrigerator and opens it. He pushes aside his Aunt "B's" green Jell-O mold then the leftovers of a tasty pheasant that he had the other night so that he can grab the milk.

Darnel goes back to the kitchen table with the milk and cereal. As he pours the milk into his bowl of cereal,

Darnel hears his dog yelp. Darnel stops pouring the milk and listens for Tyson.
"Dumb ass dog. That rabbit probably scared the shit out of you." Darnel talks to Tyson as if he were in the kitchen with him.
When Darnel doesn't hear anything from Tyson, he gets up to check on his little dog.
Darnel looks out the window above the sink. When he doesn't see Tyson, Darnel opens the back door.
A chilly winter breeze blows into the opened doorway.
Darnel hollers for Tyson. "TYSON!" Darnel listens for a second then hollers for his dog again. "TYSON!"
There is still no sign of Darnel's little dog, Tyson.
Darnel sighs. "Oh, what the hell. You can use the doggy door to get back in now." Darnel shuts the back door and goes to take a piss before finishing his cereal.
While in the bathroom, Darnel hears what he thinks is the doggy door opening then, closing. He shakes his head as he washes his hands. "Dumb ass dog."
As Darnel exits the bathroom, "Now see Tyson, using that doggy door wasn't so bad now, was it?"
Darnel takes a look around as he walks out of the bathroom to see if he can see Tyson anywhere.
Tyson is nowhere to be found.
Darnel walks back to the kitchen to finish his bowl of cereal. He sits down and eats one bite after another until his bowl is empty.
As he shovels the last spoonful of cereal into his mouth, Darnel uses his tongue to feel around in his mouth.
Without Darnel realizing it, a black tan rabbit quietly sets a bloody dog collar on the kitchen floor then hops over to Darnel's chair and sits behind Darnel, looking up at him.
Darnel slowly reaches into his mouth and pulls out

a long black hair from the back of his throat. He can feel the hair dragging along the back of his throat and the upper part of his mouth. Darnel gags on the hair as he pulls it out of his mouth. It takes everything he has to keep his cereal down.

The rabbit sitting behind Darnel silently shapeshifts into a young black and very shapely woman named, Twiggy.

Twiggy has long black hair that's slicked back into a high ponytail with hair that's been teased and waved.

Twiggy is wearing black lipstick and eyeliner to match. She has black nail polish on her fingers and toenails.

Twiggy is wearing a black leather, tie back corset with white stitching and an attached black sheer corset skirt that is almost see-through. She is also wearing black leather bracers that have an elaborate Celtic design cut out on each of them. The bracers are laced up and covering her wrists and forearms.

Twiggy grabs the back of Darnel's head and as she does, "It's your turn to be laid out, motherfucker." Before Darnel has time to react, Twiggy slams Darnel's head into his empty bowl, face first.

Darnel wakes up sometime later to find himself naked and hanging upside down, next to his father's light blue "54" convertible.

Darnel is suspended in the air by his father's engine hoist.

Twiggy is sitting at a workbench, putting some finishing touches on a red, silver and gold Easter egg when she hears Darnel stirring. "Well, well, well, look whos' finally awake. It's the asshole quarterback who thinks his shit doesn't stink." Twiggy gets up and walks over to Darnel. "Mother told me all about you. She says you like to get off on bullying your younger teammates."

Darnel's arms are at his side. He is tightly wrapped, several times with plastic wrap from his feet to his neck. "Mmm... Too bad you're all wrapped up. I could have some fun with you." Twiggy slowly runs her hand along Darnel's plastic wrapped ass and lower back as she hungrily licks her lips.

"WHAT THE FUCK!" Darnel panics and flails around like a fish out of water. "GET ME THE FUCK DOWN FROM HERE!" Darnel hollers.

As Darnel spins around, he sees several empty rolls of cardboard tubes that used to hold plastic wrap, lying on the garage floor.

Twiggy stands behind Darnel and stops him from spinning. "Whoa, hold on there, my chocolaty goodness. You're going to hurt yourself if you don't settle down." Twiggy smiles.

Darnel screams at Twiggy as he flails around some more. "WHO THE FUCK ARE YOU?" Darnel tries to get a good look at Twiggy. "GET ME THE FUCK DOWN OR I'M GOING TO KNOCK THAT SMILE OFF YOUR FACE, YOU BITCH!" Darnel screams at Twiggy again.

Twiggy slaps Darnel's plastic wrap covered ass. "Oh, I wish I could let you go. The things I could do with you." Twiggy walks back to the workbench and picks up the Easter egg that she was decorating and a roll of plastic wrap that's next to several other rolls of empty tubes of plastic wrap.

"FUCK YOU, YOU BLACK BITCH! I'M GOING TO FUCK YOU UP SO BAD WHEN I GET OUT OF HERE!" Darnel continues his flailing around.

"Mother said you're not one of the pack she is looking for and that she has no use for you. So, basically, you're just a useless fucking jock. Mother told me I can do whatever I want with you." Twiggy walks back to Darnel with the Easter egg and plastic wrap and squats in front of

Darnel.

With the Easter egg and plastic wrap in one hand, Twiggy grabs Darnel's hair with her free hand and aggressively jerks his head in such a way that Darnel is now forced to look at her. "You know, I was originally going to take you home to my burrow and fuck the skin off your cock. But then I thought about it, I thought about it long and hard and… we're going to do something different." Twiggy lets go of Darnel's hair.

Darnel doesn't say a word, he just stares at Twiggy with an angry look on his face.

"Do you know I used to have a family? It was me, Peter and my five children. We were a happy nest, that is until Peter and my children were hunted down and slaughtered for their meat." Twiggy starts to whimper as she tells Darnel her story. "Their feet were even cut off while they were still alive and kept for good luck."

Twiggy has a flashback to when she had a family.

Deep in the woods, a cottontail buck, a doe black tan rabbit and their five kits have made a burrow their home.

The family of rabbits are huddled together to keep warm for the night.

Just as the rabbits are about to drift off, the buck cottontail rabbit senses danger and quickly lifts his head up. He thumps his hind legs to alarm his family of nearby danger. The buck then races out of his burrow, leaving his doe and five kits behind in hopes that he may lead the danger away from his family.

Seconds after the buck leaves the burrow, a gunshot is heard followed by a loud squeal.

The black tan rabbit cautiously leaves the warmth and safety of the burrow to look for her buck. And just like when the buck left, there is a loud gunshot followed by a loud ear-piercing squeal.

Soon after the gunshot, a hand reaches into the burrow and pulls the five baby rabbits out.

The baby rabbits squeal just like their parents.

"I found the buck, but I can't find the doe in all this snow." A male hunter tells his friend as he puts the squealing baby rabbits into a sack.

"She has to be here somewhere. I know damn well that I hit her. Let's get these ones back to camp and then we'll come out later for the doe." The other hunter tells his friend.

Back at camp.

Two, one person tents have been set up in the snow with a roaring campfire just a few feet from the tents.

The five baby rabbits have been skinned and are now on a spit, cooking over the campfire with their feet cut off.

"Mmm... These little fuckers are going to taste so good." A fat, overweight hunter tells his friend as he waits for the baby rabbits. The fat hunter is drooling at the site of the baby rabbits cooking over the campfire.

A slightly skinnier hunter is holding a bloody buck rabbit in the air by his hind legs as he rips the rabbit's fur and skin off its dead body. "Yea, I wish we could have found the doe."

Off in the distance, the doe black tan rabbit hides behind a tree. One of its hind legs has been shot and is bleeding profusely.

When the doe sees what the hunters have done to her family, the doe squeals so loud and eerily that the sound sends cold chills up and down the hunters' backs and makes the hairs on their arms stand on end.

Back to the present time and day.

"And that's when a nice old lady picked me up out of the cold, wet and bloody snow. As she turned to walk away, I heard the screams of the hunters who had killed my family," Twiggy clears her throat. "Now I'm going to show your parents what I went through." Twiggy casually rubs a small circular scar on the upper part of her left calf.

Twiggy doesn't wait for Darnel to respond. Instead, she puts the plastic wrap on the ground and grabs Darnel's lower jaw and squeezes until Darnel's mouth is forced open. Twiggy puts her decorated Easter egg into Darnel's mouth and holds it in there while she picks up the plastic wrap and tightly wraps it around Darnel's head until there's several layers of plastic wrap covering his face and the Easter egg in his mouth.

Darnel wildly thrashes around, trying to scream and gasp for air but as he does, the plastic wrap is sucked in and around his Easter egg stuffed mouth and his nostrils.

Twiggy stands up and steps away from Darnel. She drops what is left of the roll of plastic wrap. "Usually, someone as fit as you could hold their breath for two minutes, maybe a little longer but the way you're carrying on…" Twiggy pauses for a moment as she squats in front of Darnel again. "I'd say you have thirty seconds until you pass out and then five to six minutes after that until you suffer from permanent brain damage."

Twiggy is enjoying watching the plastic wrap being sucked in and around Darnel's Easter Egg stuffed mouth every time he struggles for much needed air. "Imagine the look on your parents' faces when they come home to find their only son, braindead." Twiggy pauses then, "Oh well." Twiggy slaps Darnel's plastic wrapped covered cheeks. "Shit happens."

While still in her squatting position, Twiggy shapeshifts into her rabbit form and hops away, leaving Darnel by himself.

6

THE HARVEST

In the deepest, darkest, and coldest bowels of Tranquil Hospital, there exists a floor that no one dare not step foot on. A floor that's eerily quiet and smells of death. It's a floor everyone in the city eventually visits whether they want to or not.

The morgue in Tranquil Hospital is cold, dark, damp and eerily silent any hour of the day or night. It's the kind of silence that'll make the hairs on the back of your neck stand on end and give you goose bumps from one end of your arm to the other.

The morgue's stainless-steel door begins to frost over and keeps going until it's totally covered in ice crystals from top to bottom.

A younger Holly steps through the ice-covered door with the hood of her powder blue capelet covering her head.

Eggnog follows behind Holly, carrying a two-gallon galvanized bucket.

Holly stops and takes her hood off as she looks around the morgue. "The son of a bitch is in here somewhere. Open all the cold chambers until he is found."

"Yes mother." Eggnog responds as he walks off to another part of the morgue with his bucket.

Holly opens a door to one of the cold chambers and slides out the body that's in it. Holly pulls off the white sheet that's covering the body and lets the sheet fall to the ground.

The corpse that is under the sheet isn't who Holly is looking for so she goes on to the next cold chamber. But, as she reaches for the handle to open the door of another cold chamber, an autopsy technician walks in from a side office.

The autopsy technician puts his hands on his hips. "What the fuck! How the hell did you get in here? The door is locked." The technician motions to the door with his head, the same door that Holly and Eggnog had come through a short while ago.

Holly keeps her back to the technician and doesn't say a word.

The autopsy technician takes a few steps towards Holly then grabs one of her shoulders. "I said…"

Before the technician finishes his sentence, Eggnog walks up behind him and smashes his galvanized bucket into the technician's face so hard that an imprint of the technician's face is left in the bucket.

"No one touches mother." Eggnog says in a stern voice.

The technician's eyes roll to the back of his head. His body stiffens. He then falls back onto the cold marble floor, unconscious. His nose is flat against his face with blood oozing out of his mouth and nostrils.

Holly looks at the unconscious autopsy technician then turns to Eggnog.

The two of them exchange satisfying, mischievous smiles.

"I found the fucker." Holly puts a hand out for Eggnog's bucket.

Eggnog places the handle of his bucket in Holly's

hand.

Holly takes the bucket then turns back around to the cold chamber that she was about to open before she was rudely interrupted. She opens the cold chamber and reads the name on the corpse's toe tag. "Morris Hand."

Eggnog kneels down beside the unconscious technician and forces open his mouth. He then takes a stainless-steel dental mallet out from his belt, around his waist.

Eggnog holds the dental mallet high over the technician's head. Then, in one swift motion, Eggnog brings his mallet down onto the technician's mouth, smashing all his teeth. Eggnog does this several times until he has the technician's molar.

Once Eggnog has the molar, with great satisfaction, he puts it in a small brown, leather pouch on his belt.

Holly whips back the white sheet covering the corpse. She then places the bucket on the floor, off to the side where the corpse's head would be. Holly jerks the corpse's head and neck so that some of the corpse's neck is hanging over the bucket that she had placed on the floor.

Holly next reaches over and picks up a scalpel off a nearby table.

Without hesitation, Holly slices open the corpse's jugular then tosses the scalpel across the room.

Blood slowly dribbles out of the corpse's jugular and into the bucket on the floor.

"Another one down, many more to go." Holly tells Eggnog with a smile that stretches from one side of her face to the other.

7

FATHER MURPHY'S TWISTED CONFESSION

It's been forty-five minutes since the last of the church's congregation emptied out of the church for the night.
    The same short and stout, sixty-year-old priest who was conducting a funeral earlier in the week, walks out of a room in the back of the church. He smooths out his cassock that he is still wearing.
    A seven-year-old altar boy slowly walks out soon after the priest with his head down. The little boy's clothes are disheveled. His face is red and blotchy. And his eyes, red and puffy, as if he were crying.
    Another priest walks out behind the little boy with a little pep to his step. The priest reaches down and squeeze the boy's ass.
    The boy's ass feels so good in the priest's hand that a soft moan escapes from the priest's lips. "Mmmmh"
    The little boy tries to pull away from the priest's unwanted advances, but he cannot. The priest's hand is stuck to the boy's ass like glue.
    Once out in the open, the priest winks at the little boy then let's go of the boy's ass and makes his way to the front of the church.

The little boy keeps his head down as he walks by the first priest. He sniffles and wipes his nose on the sleeve of his arm.

The little boy's mother greets the second priest as he walks by. "Goodnight, Father Donovan."

Without saying a word, Father Donovan nods to the boy's mother then continues walking out of the church.

The first priest messes the little boy's hair as he walks by. "That's enough for today, Robert. Wonderful job. I'll see you next Wednesday." The priest smiles.

Robert lifts his head up and notices his mother standing near the entrance of the church. Robert runs to his mother as fast as he can, with open arms.

The priest notices Robert's mother standing by the front of the church, waiting for her son. "Hello, Mrs. Stephens." The priest waves.

Mrs. Stephens waves back.

When Robert reaches his mother, he slams into her side, just about knocking her over. Robert hugs his mother as tight as he can.

Robert's mother puts an arm around Robert not realizing what had just taken place between her son and the two priests. She waves back. "Hello Father Murphy."

With her arm around her son, Mrs. Stephens and Robert walk out of the church.

Father Murphy watches mother and son walk out of his church. Then as he turns to walk back to the room he had come out of, Father Murphy hears a jingle bell then notices a door to one of the confessional booths close.

Father Murphy looks at the confessional booths with a puzzled expression. He doesn't remember seeing anyone walking into the church other than Robert's mother.

Father Murphy thinks for a moment then, not wanting to keep whoever is in the confessional waiting, he makes his way over to the confessional booths.

Father Murphy enters the center compartment and shuts the door behind him. He sits down and turns on a dim light, overhead.

A sharp and sweet scent of pine fills the confessional.

Father Murphy closes his eyes and breathes in deeply.

Father Murphy is transported to a wintery dream world of pine trees and snow as far as the eye can see.

There is a light fluffy snow fall coming down.

A few more minutes and the sun will be gone, making way for the moon.

A slight breeze blows across Father Murphy's face. He enjoys the fresh scent of the pine trees.

A female's voice whispers in Father Murphy's ear. "Nicolas Murphy."

The refreshing smell of the pine trees has Father Murphy in such a euphoric trance that he doesn't hear the woman calling his name at first.

Just a few feet in front of Father Murphy are two old and weathered signs that are nailed to wooden posts with a bit of snow on them. The first one is a 12 x 8 wooden sign that reads, "Warning. This property is protected by a highly trained donkey."

Father Murphy finds the warning sign a bit funny and chuckles.

The second sign has green pine trees silhouetted on it with a white background. The font on the sign is in green and red.

The sign is old and weathered but Father Murphy is able to make out what is says. He reads the sign to himself. "Kringle family tree farm. Choose n-cut. Christmas trees."

As he finishes reading the sign, Father Murphy now hears the woman whispering in his ear.

"Father Murphy." The woman whispers in Father Murphy's ear.

Father Murphy turns to his right, where he heard the woman whispering and as he does, Father Murphy sees a beautiful white reindeer cow disappear among the pine trees.

Father Murphy decides to see where the reindeer disappeared to. When he reaches the spot where he saw the reindeer disappear into, all Father Murphy sees are more pine trees.

Father Murphy listens as he quickly looks around wondering where the reindeer went, but he hears and sees nothing. The reindeer's tracks can't even be seen.

Father Murphy has got a puzzled look on his face as he talks to himself. "Where in the world did it go? It was right here."

Father Murphy hears the woman whisper his name again, this time in his left ear.

As he quickly turns to his left, Father Murphy sees the reindeer up ahead.

The reindeer looks at Father Murphy then disappears again, into the pine trees.

Father Murphy hurries as fast as he can through the snow to where he again saw the reindeer. But as before, when he reaches the spot where he saw the reindeer for the second time, there is no sign of a reindeer.

Father Murphy lowers his head and sighs. He takes a deep breath and holds it for a second or two, enjoying the warm and refreshing smell of the pine trees and the cold winter air.

Father Murphy hears something walking through the snow. As he quickly lifts his head up, he sees the ass end of a white reindeer disappear into a grove of pine trees.

Father Murphy takes off running before the reindeer can get very far. When he reaches the grove of trees where the reindeer went into, he follows.

The grove of pine trees open up into a clearing and to Father Murphy's surprise, in the middle of the clearing is a Kondo Teak Platform Bed with bedsheets as white as the snow around it.

The bed is surround by holly and red poinsettias. There is also white fairy lights illuminating the whole bed.

But what really surprises Father Murphy is the pale, naked woman lying on the bed with one of her hands between her legs, pleasuring herself while tantalizing one of her erect nipples with her other hand.

Father Murphy watches the woman intently.

Even though he is a man of God, Father Murphy's eyes widen with excitement. He can't remember the last time he has seen the bare flesh of a woman. "Oh my." He whispers.

As Father Murphy continues to watch the woman on the bed, he hears a jingle bell coming from the grove of pine trees off to his far left.

When Father Murphy turns his head to look, the white reindeer that he was following walks out of the grove of pine trees and into the clearing.

The reindeer slowly walks towards the bed.

The woman on the bed is so into rubbing one out that she doesn't seem to be bothered that a reindeer is making its way towards her.

The reindeer stops a few feet from the foot of the bed and lifts its head up to smell the cold winter air. The reindeer then looks to where Father Murphy is hiding among the pine trees.

When Father Murphy sees the reindeer look his way he quickly ducks behind a pine tree so that he isn't discovered.

The reindeer cautiously watches the pine trees where Father Murphy is hiding. When the reindeer doesn't

see anything, it wags its tail then turns back to the bed.
As the reindeer takes a few more steps towards the foot of the bed, it rears up onto its hind legs. As the reindeer stands upright, it shapeshifts into a naked, pale skinned woman with long platinum blond hair.

The woman's name is Prancer which makes the woman on the bed, Vixen

Father Murphy cannot believe his eyes. Not only is there a bed in the middle of a snow covered clearing of pine trees with a naked woman on it, pleasuring herself, but now a reindeer magically turns into another pale skinned woman that looks identical to the woman on the bed.

Prancer steps up onto the foot of the bed then slowly slinks her way between Vixen's legs.

Vixen continues to pleasure herself as her sister slowly and seductively kisses the inside of her legs as she works her way up to her sister's crotch.

Vixen takes her hand away from between her legs and grabs the bed sheets with both hands. She arches her back with intense excitement as her sister reaches her crotch.

Prancer slowly runs her tongue around the walls of Vixen's vagina, making sure to get every fold, stopping here and there to gently bite down.

Vixen bites her bottom lip and moans as she is now holding Prancer's head between her legs.

With her tongue deep inside Vixen's vagina, Prancer doesn't seem to mind having her head held between her sister's legs.

Vixen wraps one of her legs around Prancer's back and curls her toes as Prancer continues to stimulate every tasty inch of Vixen's pink pearl.

Father Murphy is gawking at the two women having sex. He is drooling from both sides of his mouth. "Oh, my Lord." He whispers.

Father Murphy shifts his weight in the snow as he positions himself to get a better view of the two women on the bed.

Vixen hears the snow crunching under someone's foot. In her excitement, Vixen turns her head to where she heard the snow crunching.

Father Murphy again, hides behind a pine tree so that he isn't seen.

Vixen doesn't see anyone but she knows someone is watching her sister and her. Vixen smiles then closes her eyes and goes back to enjoying the loving sensation of her sister's face and tongue between her legs.

Father Murphy hears a woman whispering his name in his ear again. "Nicolas Murphy."

This time, Father Murphy awakens from his winter wonderland dream to find that he is in a confessional booth.

The woman's voice calls for Nicolas Murphy again from an adjoining confessional booth. "Nicolas Murphy."

Father Murphy apologizes to the woman. "Oh my. I'm sorry. My mind was wondered for a moment. Yes, I'm Nicolas Murphy but, you can call me Father Murphy."

For a moment, there is silence then, "You know, me and my sister once had two fathers and two mothers." The woman's voice starts to crack as if she were going to cry. "That changed though when a hunter took the life of our birth parents when me and my sister were just calves."

With a puzzled look, Father Murphy looks at the screen separating the two confessional booths and interrupts the woman. "Excuse me?"

Because of the screen separating the two confessional booths and the dim lighting, Father Murphy cannot make out the woman's features, but he can see that she has turned her head to look at him.

The woman has a flashback of her life of long ago. Two reindeer calves are huddled together in a small snowbank. They are cold and starving.

"Our mother and father left my sister and I huddled together while they led a group of hunters away from us. They never came back so, we were left trying to keep warm in the cold wet snow when a toy maker and his wife found us." The woman explains.

An elaborately decorated sleigh pulled by two reindeer stops a few feet from the reindeer calves. A heavyset older man wearing red velvet clothes steps down from the sleigh. The old man's wife follows behind him.

The old man and his wife gently pick up the reindeer calves.

Present time, inside the confessional booths.

The woman continues her story. "The toy maker and his wife took us in and raised us as if we were one of their own. They became the mother and father we didn't have. But then, like my birth father, the toy maker, our second father was taken from me and my sister by a hunter's bullet."

The woman remembers back to when she and her sister lost their father for the second time.

"Our father heard something that we didn't hear, so he told the both of us to run." The woman sniffles a bit then continues her story. "So, we did as we were told and we ran. As me and my sister ran though, we heard several gunshots. As I ran, I turned around and saw my father lying in the snow. He was the first to go down then the rest of my sisters, one by one. That was the last time we saw our sisters and our father for the second time."

"Me and my sister didn't stop until we arrived home, crying in our mother's arms. So, you are neither one of my fathers."

Father Murphy hears the woman sniffle as if she is crying. He then tries to console the woman. "I'm sorry my child. I did not…"

The woman abruptly cuts Father Murphy off before he finishes what he is saying. "Oh no, no, no, Nicolas Murphy. I think you have this all wrong. I'm not here to give you my confession."

Father Murphy has got a puzzled look on his face. "Excuse me, my child?"

The woman turns to looks at Father Murphy. She moves closer to the screen that separates the two confessional booths. "I… am… not… your child. And you, Nicolas Murphy, can call me Prancer."

Snowflakes start to magically fall inside the confessional booth that Father Murphy is in.

Father Murphy holds a handout and watches in amazement as the snowflakes lands in the palm of his hand. Father Murphy then looks up at the ceiling of the confessional where the snowflakes are coming from.

The snowflakes seem to be appearing out of thin air as the temperature in the confessional booth drops.

Father Murphy can now see his breath as he exhales.

Along with the sweet refreshing pine scent, there is now a spicy-hot cinnamon aroma in the air.

Vixen magically appears in the same confessional booth as Father Murphy. She sits on Father Murphy's lap with one of her arms around his neck and her other hand touching his chest.

Vixen is totally naked except for her white lace choker that has a silver jingle bell and a nun's wimple.

As surprised as Father Murphy is, if he could have, he would have jumped out of his confessional booth.

Vixen pats Father Murphy's chest. "Oh, Nicolas Murphy, you dirty man. Is that a cross in your pocket or are you happy to see me?"

Vixen and Prancer giggle.

Vixen rubs the back of Father Murphy's head.

"We're here for your fucking confession, you dirty pervert."

Without saying a word, Father Murphy follows the lines of Vixen's naked body all the way up to her smiling face.

In the blink of an eye, Vixen grabs the hair on the back of father Murphy's head and then with her other hand, Vixen grabs his chin and twists Father Murphy's head 180°.

The doors to the confessional booths fly open.

Standing in front of the confessional booths is Twiggy, Cupid and Pepper.

"Come my sisters. It is time to get the other pervert." Twiggy motions for Prancer and Vixen to follow as they all turn and walk away.

8

WHACK-A-MOLE

Just like clockwork, without fail, every Wednesday after church, Father Donovan stops at his favorite coffee shop, The Timepiece, for his large triple-triple before going home.

The Timepiece is decorated in a steampunk theme. There's polished dark wood and brass filigree everywhere. The deep orange and brown colored walls are decorated with all kinds of cogs, gears, and copper accents. There are also clocks of all kinds, old and new decorating the walls and shelves. A few cuckoo clocks hang from the walls, here and there. Round copper tables and wrought iron chairs are neatly scattered around the coffee shop. In the middle of the room there is also a six-foot, Indian black walnut coffee table with a copper epoxy river going down the middle of the coffee table with a matching bench on either side.

If you close your eyes, with all the copper and brass in the coffee shop, you can smell the slight aroma of metallic in the air. You can also smell coffee brewing somewhere in The Timepiece.

You can hear the ticking sound of the clocks as the seconds pass.

Father Donovan has been coming to The Timepiece for so long that he knows all the workers and customers who frequent the coffee shop by name and they know him by name as well.

Tonight though, things have changed. Father Donovan walks into The Timepiece, ready to return all the greetings but as he steps foot into the coffee shop, he notices that all the lights in the coffee shop have been turned down, making it hard to get a good look at anyone. From what Father Donovan can see, The Timepiece is empty. No customers and no employees, at least the regular employees that usually greet him as soon as he walks through the door.

Father Donovan looks around the coffee shop.

For a place that is normally filled with laughter and all kinds of conversation, The Timepiece is unusually quiet tonight.

On top of smelling coffee brewing and the slight metallic aroma in the air, Father Donovan also smells a strong scent of pine and cinnamon, something he hasn't smelt in The Timepiece before.

In a dark far corner of the coffee shop, Father Donovan notices two women wearing what looks to be white gothic trench coats and white leather, high platform boots.

The women have no expression on their faces as they watch Father Donovan make his way into the coffee shop with their hands moving back and forth under the table.

Father Donovan quickly looks away when he hears soft moans coming from the women.

"Good afternoon, Father Donovan." A dark-skinned woman with teased and wavy hair that's been put into a high ponytail speaks to Father Donovan from behind the coffee shop's counter.

Father Donovan walks to the counter while digging in his back pocket for his wallet. As he reaches the counter and the woman behind it, he finally pulls out his wallet.

The woman behind the counter greets Father Donovan with a big smile and a large triple-triple, just the way he likes it.

Father Donovan hands the woman a five-dollar bill with a smile.

The woman turns Father Donovan's money down. "Oh no, Father Donovan. It's on the house." The woman hands Father Donovan his coffee.

While still holding the money out, "Are you sure?" Father Donovan asks the woman.

"Oh yes, Father Donovan. For you, it's free." The woman smiles from ear to ear.

Father Donovan puts his money back into his wallet and returns his wallet to his back pocket. He then takes his free coffee from the woman. "Thank you." His fingers gently touching hers as the woman hands the coffee to him.

Father Donovan feels his heart racing faster. His stomach is filled with butterflies. There's even a semi growing in his pants.

Father Donovan might be a man of the cloth, but he still appreciates the beauty of a woman, especially a woman of color.

Now, Father Donovan's smile is just as big as the woman's smile, behind the counter.

The woman pulls her hand back as soon as Father Donovan has his coffee.

Father Donovan is quiet as his eyes are drawn to the woman's large breasts that are hidden behind her smock and the rest of her clothing.

The woman notices Father Donovan's attention is drawn elsewhere. She looks down at her chest then back to Father Donovan who is still fixated on her chest area.

"Do you see anything else you like, Father Donovan?" The woman asks with a mischievous smile.

The woman gently touches Father Donovan's hand that's holding the coffee.

Father Donovan realizes that he's staring at the woman's breasts and quickly looks at her name tag. The name on the name tag reads, "Twiggy".

"I haven't seen you around here before. Are you new?" Father Donovan asks the woman.

Twiggy quickly looks down at her name tag then back to Father Donovan. "Oh yes. Caroline and everyone else came down with some kind of virus so, the owners called me in from one of the other shops up North."

"Oh dear. That's terrible. I hope everyone gets better soon." Father Donovan takes a sip of his triple-triple.

"I'm sure it won't be long before they're dying to get back to work." Twiggy says as she takes a rag out of her smock pocket and wipes down the counter.

Unknown to Father Donovan, the heel of Twiggy's boot is stuck deep in Caroline's bloody throat, who is lying dead on the floor.

"Well, it's been a pleasure meeting you, Twiggy. I hope we can meet again." Father Donovan takes his coffee and walks to the front door.

"Oh, I'm sure our paths will cross again." Twiggy says as she watches Father Donovan walk away.

On his way to the front door, Father Donovan hears whispers and childish laughter coming from the two women in the corner of the coffee shop.

When Father Donovan reaches the front door of the coffee shop, he looks back at the two women in the corner.

The women are giggling and whispering in each other's ear as they watch Father Donovan. They wave to Father Donovan.

Not knowing what to make of the two peculiar women in the corner, Father Donovan decides to just open the door, nod to Twiggy, and then walk out.

Father Donovan shuts the door behind him.

As father Donovan walks by The Timepiece's big picture window, he notices all the lights are now off and there is no sign of anyone ever being in The Timepiece, Twiggy or the two women in the corner.

"What?" Father Donovan says to himself with a puzzled look. He thinks for a moment. Wondering where the people in the coffee shop had disappeared to. When Father Donovan cannot think of any solution, he continues home.

On his way down the sidewalk, Father Donovan waves to a few people from church.

The people return the greeting. "Hello father."

Father Donovan arrives at his house sometime later, a bit drowsy. With what's left of his coffee in one hand, Father Donovan sticks his house key into his door lock with his other hand.

Just as Father Donovan turns the key in the lock, his front door whips open.

"Hello, Father Donovan. I told you our paths would cross again." Twiggy says as she stands in the doorway with a mischievous looking smile.

Twiggy is wearing knee high, black leather boots, a black lace bra and a black leather tie back corset with white stitching and an attached black corset skirt that is just about see through. Twiggy is also wearing black, leather bracers with an elaborate Celtic cut-out design in them.

Father Donovan doesn't know what to say about Twiggy greeting him from inside his house and wearing what she is wearing so, he just stands and stares at Twiggy with his mouth wide open.

Father Donovan takes a quick look at what's left of his coffee then back to Twiggy who is still smiling mischievously at him.

"I see you're enjoying your coffee. How do you like the little extra TLC I put in it?" Twiggy asks then giggles. Father Donovan looks at his coffee again. Then, as he looks at Twiggy, Father Donovan's eyes roll to the back of his head followed by him falling forward into his house.

Some time has passed since Father Donovan passed out in the entryway of his house.

Father Donovan slowly wakes up to the strong smell of cinnamon and pine filling his nose. He then hears the sound of two people kissing and moaning.

Father Donovan tries to sit up, but he is unable to as he soon realizes that he is in his bed with a blanket over him and his arms and legs tied to each corner of the bed.

When Father Donovan cannot sit up, he tries to open his mouth and scream for help but because of the spine of his Bible is stuffed in his mouth with his mouth taped shut around the Bible with duct tape, he cannot say a word.

The only light in Father Donovan's bedroom is that coming from the moon which is being filtered through a partially opened window shade.

The light from the moon is casting shadows on Father Donovan's reading chair in the far end corner of his bedroom.

Father Donovan lifts his head up to see who is making the kissing and moaning sounds.

At the far end corner of Father Donovan's bedroom where the shadows are being cast onto his reading chair, Prancer and Vixen are naked and making out in Father Donovan's reading chair.

Prancer is sitting on Vixen's lap with her arms and legs wrapped around Vixen's back.

Vixen's hands are firmly gripping each one of Prancer's ass cheeks.

Prancer and Vixen have got their tongues down each other's throat. Their sweaty bodies are glistening in the moonlight.

Prancer archers her back as one of Vixen's hands slowly slips deep into the crack of her ass.

Father Donovan watches the two naked women in his reading chair.

Prancer and Vixen ignores Father Donovan while they continue their make out session.

Out of frustration, Father Donovan lets his head drop back onto his pillow. He tries to maneuver the Bible out of his mouth but it's no use, Father Donovan's mouth has been closed and secured so tightly around the Bible that his teeth are biting into the Bible.

Father Donovan lets out a sigh as drool runs out the side of his mouth. He closes his eyes as he is forced to listen to the two women kiss and moan.

"You like that, don't you father? Two women having their way with each other." Twiggy slowly slithers out of the darkness of one of the corners of Father Donovan's bedroom, by his headboard.

Father Donovan is startled. He quickly lifts his head up and watches as Twiggy gets closer.

"And that odor my two sisters give off when they're excited." Twiggy pauses for a second and closes her eyes. She bites her bottom lip. "Mmm… It's quite intoxicating." Twiggy breathes in deeply as she refers to the strong pine and cinnamon odor filling Father Donovan's bedroom.

Twiggy opens her eyes and makes her way to Father Donovan's bedside and as she does, Twiggy glances down at a framed picture of Mother Teresa on Father Donovan's nightstand. She picks the picture up and continues walking to the foot of Father Donovan's bed.

When Twiggy reaches the foot of Father Donovan's bed, she turns around on her heels to face Father Donovan.

"Oh wait. Silly me. You don't like women do you father? It's the flesh of the young and innocent that you hunger for." Twiggy pauses for a moment to look at the picture of Mother Teresa. She then looks into the horror-stricken eyes of Father Donovan. "You like to play a little game called cornhole, don't you father?"

Cupid bursts into Father Donovan's bedroom, holding a stainless steel, meat mallet. "Eeew! That's disgusting."

Pepper walks in behind Cupid, sucking on a candy cane. Pepper takes the candy cane out of her mouth and whispers in Cupid's ear. "What is cornhole?"

While making a hand gesture towards her ass as if something were going in and out of it, Cupid explains to Pepper what cornhole is.

Pepper quickly looks at Father Donovan with an ugly, disgusted look on her face. "Oooh! You sick crusty son of a bitch."

By now, the twins have finished their little make out session in Father Donovan's reading chair and are getting dressed.

Cupid and Pepper stand on one side of Father Donovan's bed while the twins are positioning themselves on the other side with Twiggy at the foot of the bed.

The five women smile at each other. They then turn to look at a horror-stricken Father Donovan.

"Now for the reason why we're all here." Twiggy grabs the blanket that's covering Father Donovan and yanks it off him. Twiggy then let's the blanket fall to the floor, behind her.

Father Donovan is completely naked, except for the excessive hair covering his plump body. You would think he was some kind of animal with all the hair on his body.

Four of the five women are laughing at the sight of Father Donovan's plump, hairy body while Twiggy stands

at the foot of the bed, not saying a word.
    Father Donovan tries to scream again but still cannot.
    Twiggy is distracted from her train of thought as she glances down at Father Donovan's limp, tiny penis. A childish giggle escapes her lips. "Oh, now I see why you like to go fishing for brown trout with your altar boys. No woman in her right mind would want something that small."
    All five women laugh hysterically.
    Father Donovan thrashes around, hoping he might escape.
    Cupid hands Twiggy the meat mallet.
    "I suggest you calm yourself down and pray to your God for forgiveness, because no one is going to hear you scream. And there is no way in hell you're getting out of here alive." Twiggy says as she aggressively jams the picture of Mother Teresa under Father Donovan's hairy scrotum sack.
    Father Donovan takes in a deep breath through his nose. His eyes widen with fear. Father Donovan's body is starting to emit a pungent cheesy odor.
    "You know, I was going to kill you and end it there, but I thought about it and… Fuck. You made a game out of fucking little boys so, we're going to play a game with you called, whack-a-mole." Twiggy looks at each one of her sisters. "Ladies, time to play."
    Pepper chews and swallows what's left of her candy cane.
    Father Donovan begins to cry hysterically, to the point where he pisses himself.
    "EOW!" All five women say in unison as they look at Father Donovan's piss covered crotch.
    Twiggy grips the handle of the meat mallet tightly in her hand. "You fucking pig. You pissed all over

yourself." Twiggy says as she slams the meat mallet down onto Father Donovan's scrotum sack, smashing all of its contents with one strike.

The glass in the picture frame of Mother Teresa shatters, causing severe cuts on Father Donovan's scrotum sack.

Blood and piss now stain the bed sheet and the shattered picture of Mother Teresa.

Father Donovan's body stiffens as he screams as loud as he can.

Twiggy hands the meat mallet off to Vixen.

Vixen looks at the meat mallet with an evil grin that stretches from one side of her face to the other. She then looks at Twiggy. Then, without looking where she is striking, Vixen smashes Father Donovan's bloody and deflated scrotum sack several times.

Father Donovan's body stiffens again as he tries to scream.

Prancer, Cupid and Pepper cheer and clap with great excitement while Twiggy watches on, like a foreman supervising her workers.

Father Donovan's scrotum sack looks like a small piss and blood covered pancake.

It's Prancer's turn in their little game of whack-a-mole as she takes the bloody meat mallet from her sister.

While looking deep into Father Donovan's tear-filled eyes, Prancer takes her turn. She misses.

Instead of hitting Father Donovan's scrotum, she hits the head of Father Donovan's penis.

Father Donovan screams.

Unhappy that she missed her target the first time, Prancer howls with laughter as she quickly grips the handle of the meat mallet with both hands and wildly strikes at Father Donovan's crotch. This time, Prancer nails her target, not once but five times.

Prancer tosses the bloody meat mallet to Cupid who in return laughs hysterically as she smashes both Father Donovan's shaft and what's left of his scrotum sack.

The hairs on Pepper's body stand on end as she jumps wildly up and down. "My turn, my turn, my turn."

The women giggle as Cupid hands Pepper the meat mallet.

As soon as Pepper has the meat mallet, she brings it down hard onto Father Donovan's forehead.

Father Donovan's forehead cracks open like a walnut.

Blood flows from Father Donovan's forehead.

"Oh shit. I hit the wrong nut sack." Pepper giggles.

Father Donovan has stopped his thrashing. He is now silent and still.

After Pepper, the women continue to take turns playing their version of whack-a-mole until all that's left of Father Donovan's crotch is blood, piss, and ground beef.

When the women are done, they file out of Father Donovan's bedroom, one at a time.

Since Twiggy is the last one out, she slams the door behind her, leaving Father Donovan's lifeless body behind.

Father Donovan won't be playing cornhole anymore. Twiggy and her sisters made sure of that.

9

CHOKE N' STROKE

    A man wearing a long slightly worn, black trench coat and a beanie is walking along one of the many paths in Central Park. The man takes one last drag on the butt of his cigarette and then flicks the unwanted cigarette butt into a nearby snowbank.
    The cigarette makes a "sss" sound as it's discarded into the snow.
    The man flips up the collar on his trench coat to keep the chilly winter breeze off his neck. He then puts his hands in his coat pockets and continues walking through Central Park.
    Along the way, he passes a sleigh being pulled by a horse and its driver.
    The man comes to a park bench. He nervously looks around then brushes the snow off the park bench. When the bench is free of snow, the man then sits down and waits.
    A black tan rabbit jumping across the sidewalk catches the man's attention.
    The man watches the rabbit until it disappears somewhere behind a sturdy snow-covered tree.
    On the other side of the snow-covered tree, the man is surprised to see two women staring at him.
    The women have long platinum blond hair and pale,

silky smooth skin and not a blemish on them, not even an inch of fat.

It's not that the women are staring at him that surprises the man. It's the fact that they are naked and standing in ankle deep snow wearing just white suede boots with white fur lining and an oversized silver knitted scarf that's wrapped around their neck and head. The ends of the scarf are covering the women's breasts and crotch area.

As a few other people walk by the man on the bench, the man is also surprised that he is the only one that sees the women in the snow.

The two women wink at the man.

The man soon forgets about the women when he is just about pushed off the bench when he is bump into by a little man who is also now sitting on the park bench.

The little man is wearing tan caribou snow boots, black snow pants and a black hooded parka.

The little man's head and facial features are hidden by the parka's hood.

The man quickly looks back to where the women were standing. The women are now gone.

The man now directs his attention to the little man sitting beside him. "What the fuck! Excuse the fuck out of you!" The man is angry that he was almost pushed off the park bench and into the snow by such little person.

The little man takes the hood off his head to reveal a wrinkly, leathered face of a man with a brown goatee and lots of facial hair.

The little man looks at the man he almost knocked off the bench. "William Jay?" The little man asks in a deep raspy voice.

"Yea, and who the fuck are you?" William asks as he quickly looks around the park. "Where in the hell is Dickie?" William asks.

"So many questions, so little time." The little man

takes a few second to compose himself then, "Mr. Jenkins is a little indisposed of right now so, he sent me in his place. You can call me, Eggnog." Eggnog nods his head at William with a slight smile.

William giggles when he hears the little man's name. "What the fuck kind of name is that? Isn't that some shit you drink around Christmas time?"

"There you go with the fucking questions again. If you must know, Eggnog is the name my mother gave to me when I was born." Eggnog digs into his many pockets as he looks at William with an angry glare. "It's also the same shit that's going to fuck you up if you don't stop with the fucking questions." Eggnog pulls out a small, rolled up, brown paper bag from one of his coat pocket and hands it to William.

William takes the brown bag, opens it, and looks inside. William then quickly rolls the bag back up and stuffs it into one of his coat pockets while looking around the park. When he is satisfied that no one is around, William pulls out a small wad of money from the same pocket that he stuffed the paper bag in. He turns to give the wad of money to the little man sitting beside him but to William's surprise, the little man is gone without a trace. "What the fuck." William quickly stands up and looks around for the little man.

When he doesn't see the little man, William puts the wad of money back into his coat pocket and hurries out of Central Park before the little man comes back for the money.

A Paranoid, William occasionally looks behind him to make sure he isn't being followed. He does this all the way home.

As William approaches the 50 Street Subway Station, he notices a rabbit scurrying across a busy 8th Ave. where it darts in front of a Blue Bird bus and disappears in the pedestrian crowded sidewalk.

William is sure it's the same rabbit he seen in Central Park. He thinks about the rabbit for a second, then continues his hurried walk back to his apartment.

It's not long before William is at the front door of his apartment complex.

The thick blanket of snow does nothing to hide the type of rundown neighborhood that William lives in. There's overturned garbage cans and trash thrown everywhere. The outside appearance of William's apartment complex is that of a rundown and dilapidated building. Most of the windows are smashed and broken, allowing for the elements to enter the building. Some of the windows are even boarded up. If there were ever a fire, the tenants inside wouldn't be able to use the fire escape because it is rusted and unusable. Parts of the fire escape are even falling off.

William watches a couple police cars speed by with their lights flashing and their sirens blaring.

It may not be the Baccarat Hotel, but it is a roof over William's head.

As William approaches his apartment complex's front door, he looks down at the top stoop and sees another little man sleeping, curled up in the fetal position.

The sleeping man reeks of piss and shit. His clothes are old, dirty, tattered, and wet from the snow. The man has a knit cap pulled down snug over the back of his neck and ears. The knit cap might have been a different color at some time, but now, because of it being so dirty, the knit cap has taken on a dark, dingy brown color.

The sleeping man is also wearing one worn sneaker that looks to be a size too small and an old black work boot that is a size too big and missing the shoestrings. The boot also has a hole worn through the bottom by the heel and a hole by the man's gnarled big toe.

The sleeping man's gnarled, dirty toe is sticking out of the hole in the boot. The toenail of the man's big toe is long, black, and curled under.

"Fucking midgets. What the hell. Is there some kind of convention in town or what?" William nudges the sleeping man with his foot instead of using his hand. "Yo, little man, you alive?" William waits for a response from the sleeping man.

A few seconds later, the sleeping man stirs in his sleep, ignoring the nudge of William's foot as he rolls over with his back towards William.

Agitated that he is ignored by the little man, William pushes on the little man's lower back with his foot. "You fucking piece of shit, get the fuck off my steps."

The little man stirs again and then moans.

Getting a little more agitated, "Don't make me throw your ass off these fucking steps."

The little man stirs once more then sits up as he rubs his eyes. He then looks up at William.

Even with the knit cap on, the little man looks strangely familiar to William. William feels as if he has seen the little man before. But he can't quite place him.

The little man opens his jacket, pulls out a broken, red and white candy cane that's been partially eaten and holds it up to William. "A dollar for a candy cane, kind sir?" The little man looks up at William with a half-hearted smile and a twinkle in his eyes.

"Fuck you, you little piece of shit." William kicks the little man so hard that he falls off the stoop and into a snowbank. "And shove that candy cane up your ass."

William continues into his apartment complex without giving what he just did to the little man a second thought.

Once inside, William slams the door behind him. The hallway leading to the rooms and upper floors of the apartment complex smell of piss and some kind of rotting animal. There's also trash cluttering the hallway; discarded rotting food, papers, broken glass and dirty mattresses, mattresses you wouldn't dare sleep on unless you wanted to wake up with some kind of STD. There are also a few piles of snow that have blown in through the broken windows.

William notices two whores talking with each other while standing at the foot of the stairs, leading to the other floors.

The whores have got so much perfume on that William could smell them before he even walked through the front door of the complex.

One of the whores is wearing a purple and black, skintight leather skirt, a halter top, fish net pantyhose and red high heels.

The other whore is wearing skintight blue jeans that look as if they are painted on her and a black bra and black high heels.

The two whores are also wearing coats. One of them, an all-white, full length, white fur coat and the other whore, a fur coat with leopard print the goes to her waist.

The two whores see William and smile as they stop their talking.

As William gets closer to the women, he too smiles back with a slight head nod. "Ladies." He speaks.

The whores move to the side so that William can walk up the stairs, to his floor.

"Are we going to see you tonight, William?" One of the whores asks William as he walks past them.

William quickly plants a kiss on the cheek of one of the whores as he walks by.

The two whores giggle childishly.

William turns to the two women with a smile as he continues to walk up the stairs and blows the both of them a kiss. "Of course." He responds."

As William turns back around, a shapely but slender black woman passes William on the stairs.

William and the woman lock eyes.

The woman's hypnotic, bright blue eyes have got William in such a deep trance that everything around William has disappeared. There is only William and the woman.

Without taking their eyes off each other, the woman continues walking down the stairs while William walks up to his floor.

William bumps into a sweat and musty smelling elderly lady who is moving along down the stairs with the help of a cane.

The elderly woman falls backwards. She hollers at William as she lands on her wrinkly old ass.

William is jolted out of his hypnotic daze. He turns to look at the old woman sitting on the stairs. Surprised at what he has done, William offers to help the woman to her feet. "Oh, I'm sorry granny. I wasn't watching where I was going."

Not only is the old woman upset about being knocked down, but she is also irritated about being called granny. "Granny? Dagnabit! You younger generation have no respect for your elders." The old woman yanks her hand away from William, grunts and continues walking down the stairs.

William rolls his eyes and sighs. He then goes back to ogling over the beautiful black woman that just passed him on the stairs. When William turns to look for her, she is gone. It's just William and the old woman in the stairway.

As the old woman walks around the corner, out of view, she pops her head back around and flips William a gnarled old middle finger.

William kindly returns a middle finger to the old lady as well then turns and continues up the flight of stairs.

As William rounds the corner to go up one more flight of stairs, he notices that on every step, there are pastel colored Easter eggs. Some of the steps have more than one egg.

The eggs are also elaborately decorated with silver and gold designs while others have red and silver or red and gold designs.

William has got a puzzled look on his face. "What the fuck. Who in the hell put all these fucking eggs on the steps?"

William looks at the eggs as he slowly walks up the stairs. He smashes all the eggs along the way.

Decorated eggshells and the inside of the hard-boiled eggs lay all over the steps where they were smashed.

By the time William reaches the last step, it looks like a murder scene of Easter eggs.

A short time later, William is in his one room, low-class, ramshackle apartment. William's one room apartment has everything any other apartment or house would have; a refrigerator, kitchen sink, a toilet, a small two burner stove and a ratty old cot to sleep on.

The only difference with William's apartment is that you can sit on William's cot and still be able to reach the refrigerator, kitchen sink, stove, and the toilet without having to get up.

There are dirty clothes strewn all over. Discarded, dirty bags and papers from fast food restaurants with rotting food that's been partially eaten still in them blanket William's floor. There are also empty pill bottles lying all over with dried up tubes of superglue piled up by William's cot.

The walls of William's apartment have a filthy,

yellowish discoloration to them from years of never being cleaned and cigarette smoke. If you close your eyes and breathe in deeply, you can smell the years of cigarette smoke in the room.

A cold winter draft is finding its way into William's apartment through cracks and missing pieces of drywall.

William takes the rolled-up paper bag out of his coat pocket then takes off his coat and lets it drop among the trash on his floor.

He sits down on his cot and sets his brown paper bag beside him like a little kid at lunch time in school. William reaches under his dirty, sweat covered pillow and pulls out some rolling papers.

 A few minutes have passed.
 Just as William finishes rolling a joint, there's a knock on his apartment door.
 William looks at his freshly rolled and ready to smoke joint. He lets out a sigh then, "Who is it? I'm kind of busy right now." William waits for an answer from his unexpected guest before lighting his joint up.
 A brief moment of silence is followed by another knock on William's door.
 As William puts the joint up to his lips, "GOD DAMN IT! WHAT THE FUCK!" William sets his joint on his cot and stands up in a huff. As he walks to his door, "Ladies, when we agreed to meet, I didn't mean this early." Within one or two steps, William is already at his door. "I've got something to do first ladies. So, how about just a little bit…" William peers out the door's peephole and sees no one.
 For a second, William is puzzled as to who was knocking. Whomever it was had no time to walk away because William was at the door seconds after the second knock.

William then remembers the joint waiting for him on his cot.

As William turns to walk back to his cot, there's another knock on his door.

William stops and grunts out of frustration and throws his hands in the air. "I don't have time or patients for your games right now, ladies."

"You'll find time for us, Mr. Jay." A raspy sounding voice says from the other side of William's door.

William recognizes the voice. It's Eggnog, the little man who gave him his brown paper bag of goodies, in the park.

William quickly looks through his peephole and as he does, there is another knock. William sees the little man he met in the park and behind him, the beautiful black woman he had passed on the stairs, on the way up to his room.

The woman speaks. "You shouldn't have smashed my eggs, William. That wasn't very nice of you."

"What the fu…" William doesn't get the chance to finish is sentence.

In the blink of an eye, the black woman spins around and lands a back kick to William's door. The door explodes, sending wooden splinters inward, towards William.

William covers his face with his arms as he falls back onto his trash covered floor.

Eggnog walks into William's room with Twiggy following behind.

William panics. "Hold on, hold on. I have your money. There's no need for this." William reaches into his pants pocket.

Eggnog points a gnarly finger at William. "I don't want your fucking money." Eggnog continues walking towards William with Twiggy close behind him. "Mother

originally wanted us to drain you of your blood and bring it back to her but seeing that your blood is polluted with all those fucking drugs, there's been a change in plans.
Instead, I'm going to take what teeth you have left in your mouth, if there are any good ones left and when I'm done, my friend here is going to take your life."

  Later that night.
  The two whores that William was going to meet up with cautiously walk up to what's left of William's door.
  There are no lights on. Even though William's room is a small one room apartment, the two whores cannot see a thing inside William's apartment with it being so dark.
  One of the whores slowly but cautiously sticks her head in. "Hello? William? It's Jules and Tabatha."
  There's no answer.
  The whores take a step or two into William's room. One of them finds a light switch and flips the switch on.
  William's one room apartment is illuminated as the light flickers to stay on.
  The whores soon find out why William wasn't answering them.
  There, in front of them, naked and hanging from the light fixture by an electrical cord fashioned into a noose is William. His body is rigid and cold. William's toothless mouth is still gushing blood. The index finger of William's left hand has been superglued into his asshole while his right hand is superglued to the shaft of his penis.
  The whores' screams are heard throughout the apartment complex.

10

DOUBLE VISION

6A.M.

All is quiet in Rock City State Forest, Cattaraugus, New York.

A light fluffy snowfall in coming down, covering everything in a fresh, white powdery blanket.

On one side of Rock City State Forest, two beautiful white reindeer cows are foraging for an early morning meal on the snow-covered ground.

If it weren't for a few patches of light brown fur and black markings around their eyes, nose, mouth and felt covered antlers, the reindeer cows would have blended in with their snow-covered surroundings.

On the other side of Rock City State Forest, Austin and his eight-month pregnant wife, Brittany are dressed from head to toe in white camouflage clothing to blend in with the rest of the snow-covered forest.

Austin and Brittany are trying to be as quiet as possible as they make their way through some thick, snow-covered brush while wearing snowshoes.

Both Austin and Brittany have a rifle slung over their shoulders. Austin is carrying a Winchester model 70 Alaskan Rifle while Brittany has a Ruger Hawkeye

Alaskan Rifle.

As the couple approach the opening of a cave, Austin stops and listens for any noise coming from inside the cave.

Brittany stops and whispers to Austin. "What's wrong?"

Austin quickly turns around and motions for his wife to be quiet then points to the cave.

They both hear snoring sounds coming from inside the cave.

Austin and Brittany unshoulder their rifles.

Meanwhile, on the opposite side of the forest, the two reindeer cows are still eating when off in the distance, they hear a loud "BOOM! BOOM!"

The reindeer cows stop their eating and quickly raise their heads up to listen.

Another "BOOM!" is heard.

Startled, the reindeer take off running through the forest.

Austin and Brittany have gotten what they came for, a one hundred and seventy-five-pound female black bear. And as an added bonus, two, two-week-old cubs.

As Brittany carelessly tosses the dead cubs into the bed of her husband's truck, one at a time, as if they were rag dolls she no longer has any use for, "Holy shit. I can't believe I got my first black bear." Brittany tells Austin with great excitement.

As Austin walks by his excited wife, he stops long enough to give her a kiss on her lips then, "Yea, you nailed that fucker before it even opened its eyes and realized we were in its den." Austin laughs as if he found something funny in what he just said. "It's going to make for a great throw rug in our living room." Austin tells Brittany.

Unknown to Austin and Brittany, a woman with platinum blond hair is watching them through the trees and thick foliage as they load the black bear and her cubs onto the truck.

"And the cubs will make for some soft and comfy pillows next to the fireplace once they're stuffed." With a big mile, Brittany nods her head to Austin.

With the help of a winch mounted in the bed of his truck, Austin drags the one hundred and seventy-five-pound bear up a makeshift ramp and into the bed of his truck.

A tree branch snaps off in the distance.

Austin hears the snap of the tree branch and stops winching the bear into his truck so that he can listen for what made the tree branch snap.

Except for the sound of a slight wintery breeze blowing, all is quiet in Rock City State Forest.

A somewhat sweet and spicy aroma fills Austin's nose as he takes a deep breath in through his nose. He smells cinnamon.

"What's wrong, honey?" Brittany asks Austin.

Austin listens for a few more seconds before answering his wife. "Oh, it was nothing. I thought I heard something." Austin sniffs the air. "Do you smell that?" Austin pauses then, "It smells like cinnamon."

Brittany shrugs her shoulders, not saying a word.

The cinnamon smell disappears.

"Oh well." Austin goes back to winching the black bear into his truck.

Brittany wipes the cubs' blood she got on her hands, off in the snow as best as she can.

Once the black bear and her cubs are loaded and secure in Austin's truck, Austin next hitches his snowmobile trailer to the trailer hitch on the bumper of his truck. Then he loads the snowmobile that he used to drag the dead black bear back to his truck, onto the trailer.

Brittany stands by and watches her husband as she rubs her round pregnant belly. "You're going to be a big game hunter just like your daddy." Brittany talks to the baby in her belly.

Sometime later, after everything has been loaded into Austin's truck and snowmobile trailer, Austin and Brittany are finally on their way home from their little hunting trip.

Austin occasionally glances over at his wife as she is looking down at her round belly, gently rubbing it.

Austin takes his eyes off the road for a second to join his wife in showing their unborn child some affection by rubbing Brittany's belly as well.

Brittany feels the baby kicking. She looks at Austin with an excited look. "Did you feel that? He kicked."

Austin quickly looks to where he is driving then back to his excited wife who has the biggest smile he has ever seen,

They are both excited about their soon to be new arrival.

Brittany glances up at the road ahead of them and there, to her surprise, standing in the middle of the road is an adult, white reindeer cow.

The reindeer lifts its head up and looks at the truck speeding towards her. The reindeer doesn't budge.

"AUSTIN, A DEER IN THE ROAD!" Brittany points in front of her as she hollers to Austin.

"HOLY SHIT!" Austin slams on his brakes. His truck and snowmobile trailer fishtails on the snow-covered road before coming to a stop, inches from hitting the reindeer cow.

The reindeer still doesn't move an inch, even after the truck has stopped inches from it.

The reindeer curiously watches the truck's passengers.

Austin has both hands white knuckled around the steering wheel. He rests his head on the driver's headrest and closes his eyes while letting out a huge sigh of relief. "Holy shit." Austin then opens his eyes and looks at his terrified wife. "You guys okay?" Referring to Brittany and their child.

Brittany has both hands on the dashboard. Her arms are fully extended and locked in place. She slowly turns to Austin. "Fuck, I almost had a heart attack. I think I might have even pissed myself."

Austin takes a double take at the reindeer that's still watching them.

The reindeer looks away a few times and sniffs the winter air.

"What the hell, that's no ordinary deer, honey. That's a fucking reindeer cow. Look at its antlers. They've got to be at least twenty inches long." Austin is amazed at the reindeer standing in front of his truck.

With her hands now on her belly, "She's still not moving." Brittany refers to the reindeer.

Austin gets an idea. "You know… you got the bear, I'm going to get myself this fucker, standing in front of us." Austin slowly reaches for his door handle.

From out of the driver's side of the window, off in the forest, Brittany sees something running towards Austin's truck.

Brittany quickly taps Austin's should as he starts to open his driver's door.

Austin turns to Brittany. "What?" He asks.

Without saying a word, Brittany points out the driver's window.

Austin turns his head and sees another white reindeer cow. This one though is charging Austin's truck at full speed.

"HOLY SHIT! IT'S GOING TO HIT THE TRUCK!" Austin turns to Brittany and shields her face.

When the charging reindeer gets within twelve feet from Austin's truck, it leaps into the air and as it does, in one fluent movement, the reindeer shapeshifts into the form of a pale skinned woman with long platinum blond hair and black makeup.

To her friends and family, the woman is known as Vixen.

Vixen is dressed in a white lace bra and matching underwear. She has thin, white Christmas ribbon wrapped around her upper body and a white lace choker around her neck with one jingle bell. Vixen is also wearing white fishnet stockings and white leather, high platform boots that stop just below her knees and buckle all the way up.

Vixen spirals towards the driver's window, with her arms out in front of her.

The jingle bell on Vixen's white lace choker rings as she spirals towards Austin's truck.

Brittany quickly looks out towards the front of the truck, just in time to see the reindeer standing in front of the truck shapeshift into a pale skinned woman with long platinum blond hair and black makeup.

The woman is Vixen's sister, Prancer.

From Brittany's point of view, the woman is wearing a tight, white leather and lace corset that laces up and ties in the front. She is also wearing tight, white leather pants.

When Prancer looks at Brittany, Brittany notices the woman is wearing a white lace choker with a small silver jingle bell on it.

Prancer smiles and waves at Brittany.

The blink of a human eye takes 1/3 of a second. A lot can happen in the blink of an eye, sometimes life altering events.

For example…

You step off a curb to cross the road and you're struck dead by a speeding vehicle.

You arrive home after grocery shopping with your five year old daughter in the back seat. When you open your driver's door to get out and get your daughter and groceries, you're hit by a lightning bolt from a raging thunderstorm outside.

As you take a knee to propose to your pregnant girlfriend whom you've known since high school, you are hit in the head by a stray bullet used in a drive-by shooting.

Now take Brittany as another example.

Brittany blinks after the woman standing in front of Austin's truck smiles and waves at her.

Within the 1/3 of a second that it takes for Brittany to blink, the reindeer that was charging Austin's truck and shapeshifts into Vixen as she leaps into the air, towards Austin's truck, spirals through the driver's window, shattering the window into hundreds of pieces and then with a twist and a yank of Austin's head, Vixen decapitates Austin with her bare hands. Then without stopping, Vixen continues spiraling to the passenger side of the truck and does the same to Brittany's head.

Vixen moves so fast that she barely gets a drop of blood on her.

Vixen smashes through the passenger window and lands on her feet with Austin and Brittany's heads tucked into her arms like two footballs.

Blood from Austin and Brittany's decapitated bodies spray everywhere, inside the truck.

Vixen and Prancer smile at each other as Vixen drops Austin and Brittany's heads into a snowbank.

Prancer walks to the passenger side of the truck. She watches the blood spray out of Brittany's dead pregnant body. Prancer takes a finger and sticks it in the blood spraying out of Brittany's neck. Prancer then puts her blood covered finger in her mouth. She moans as she sucks her finger clean of all of Brittany's blood. "Mmm... The blood of a pregnant bitch tastes so good."

Both Prancer and Vixen laugh.

Prancer picks up a jagged piece of glass out of the snow and stabs it deep into Brittany's pregnant belly. She pushes the jagged glass all the way into Brittany's belly until the glass can no longer be seen.

11

MOMMY'S HERE TO SAVE THE DAY

Back in the day when Santa was alive, the reindeer barn housed eight reindeer with room to grow if need be. There was a loft above the stables that was used as living quarters for whatever elf was taking care of the reindeer at the time.

There was even a veterinary hospital connected to the barn that also served as a regular hospital for everyone in Christmas Village.

Tonight though, the lights in the barn have been turned down.

At the far end of the barn, the Nutcracker sits undisturbed and covered up with a large red velvet blanket.

Along the wall to the right of where the Nutcracker is stored, a warm fire burns in a huge rustic stone fireplace.

On either side of the barn, just before the Nutcracker, there are four empty and cleaned out stalls. Each one is made from beautiful Brazilian hardwood and wrought iron grills with a small gold nameplate on each of the stall doors that read, Dasher, Dancer, Prancer, Vixen, Comet, Cupid, Donner, and Blitzen.

The barn itself was built to withstand the test of time but its occupants, not so much. The barn has been empty and quiet for some time, except for one of the empty stalls by the fireplace, which is now home to a donkey named Nester and then Vixen's stall who she now shares with her sister, Prancer.

Prancer's nameplate has been taken off her stall and put onto Vixen's, right next to Vixen's nameplate

Vixen and Prancer are both naked and standing up in Vixen's stall. Vixen has got Prancer's back pushed against the back of her stall with their pale sweaty bodies pressed up against the other with their eyes closed.

One of Prancer's hands is on Vixen's upper back while her other hand slowly moves to Vixen's lower back.

Vixen gently squeezes her sister's pale ass with both hands.

The cinnamon and pine odor in the barn is so strong, you can taste it.

Prancer and Vixen moan as they take turns sucking on each other's tongue as if it were a piece of sweet tasty candy, while exchanging saliva in the process.

Vixen bites Prancer's bottom lip as one of her hands slides into the crack of Prancer's ass.

Prancer moans a little louder as Vixen's fingers work their way, deep into her crack.

Unknown to the twins, the large barn door slowly and quietly slides open.

Mr. Heat sticks his head in and looks around. His long, bright red hair is unkept and sticking up everywhere. Some of the snow that is falling has found its way into Mr. Heat's messy hair but quickly melts and turned into steam as it hits his head. Mr. Heat's thick bushy eyebrows look like frost bitten caterpillars.

Mr. Heat looks to the far end of the barn where the fireplace is on the right side. He sees Nester's stall. "Fucking jackass gets treated better than I do." Mr. Heat says to himself.

Mr. Heat then looks up at the loft on the left side of

the barn. He sees Twiggy's six foot tall snowshoe rabbit statue or as Twiggy would call it, her pleasure pod. With help from Frostbite, Twiggy had her pleasure pod moved from her room in the main living quarters to the loft some time ago.

Mr. Heat knows Twiggy is enjoying the pleasures her pod has to offer because he can hear it humming and plus she is the only one around here who dares use it.

Mr. Heat closes his eyes and breathes in deeply through his nose. He can smell the excitement in the air. Mr. Heat opens his eyes and licks the aroma on his lips.

Mr. Heat sees a roaring fire in the fireplace. He then notices the overhead lighting over one of the stalls has been turned on. Mr. Heat hears moaning coming from the same stall.

Mr. Heat decides to walk into the barn, quietly closing the barn door behind him.

Mr. Heat is wearing his black and white pinstripe suite.

Stopping a few feet into the barn, Mr. Heat closes his eyes again and sticks his nose in the air. His pale freckle covered puffy cheeks rise as his smile curls up and around.

Mr. Heat knows what the strong smell of cinnamon and pine means.

As He takes in more of the cinnamon and pine aroma, Mr. Heat licks his lips while adjusting the growing lump in his pants.

More steam rises from Mr. Heat's head as his body temperature rises.

As Mr. Heat unbuttons the first two buttons on his dress shirt, a handful of thick, bushy red chest hair pops out. He then makes sure the rest of his pinstripe suite looks presentable by flattening out any wrinkles.

When he is satisfied with the way he looks, Mr. Heat struts his cocky self over to the stall where the moaning is coming from.

Just as Mr. Heat reaches the stall, he licks the pinky and index finger of one hand and then uses those fingers to neatly press down his bushy eyebrows.

Mr. Heat looks around before approaching the stall.

When he reaches the stall, Mr. Heat reads the nameplate on the stall, "Vixen". Another nameplate has been added to the same stall, next to Vixen's nameplate, "Prancer".

Mr. Heat peers in through the wrought iron grill door.

To Mr. Heat's excitement, he sees a naked Prancer up against the back of the stall with Vixen standing in front of her, who in return is also naked.

The twins continue to moan, enjoying each other's loving touch. They are taking great pleasure in fondling each other while sticking their tongues down each other's throats. Each sister is enjoying the taste of their own sister's saliva in their mouth.

Mr. Heat puts one hand on the wrought iron grill of the stall's door and his other hand down the front of his pants where he starts to jerk himself off.

Prancer hears the stall door rattling so, she opens her eyes while keeping her tongue in Vixen's mouth.

Mr. Heat's muscles tense as he jerks himself off. His eyes roll to the back of his head.

Prancer smiles as Vixen continues to suck on her tongue. Prancer pulls away from her sister then whispers in her ear. "We have a visitor."

Vixen slowly turns around.

The twins both smile and then giggle at the same time.

"Why don't you come on in…" Prancer is the first to say something to an excited Mr. Heat.

"…and join the party little man." Vixen finishes the

sentence that her sister started.

Mr. Heat abruptly stops his masturbating and quickly takes his hand out of his pants. His eyes widen with surprise as if he were a child who had just gotten caught by his mom with his hand in the cookie jar.

"Are you going to just stand there with your hands in your pants, gawking at us…" Prancer says with a flirtatious smile.

"…or are you going to step in here and join the party?" Vixen asks sarcastically.

Mr. Heat thinks for a second while gawking at the twins from their feet to their faces then back down to their shaven and tattooed crotch. He wonders if they taste as good as they smell.

Mr. Heat has a small smile on his face as he spots the tattoo of a mistle-toe on their shaved pubic area.

The twins notice that Mr. Heat's attention is on their crotch. They turn to each other, smile then turn back to Mr. Heat.

"Do you like what you see, little man?" Both women ask as they lick an index finger then touch the same index finger to the other sister's crotch.

"Do you want to kiss us…" Vixen starts to ask.

"…under our mistletoe?" Prancer finishes Vixen's question.

The twins both flirtatiously wink at Mr. Heat.

Mr. Heat thinks for a moment, wondering if the twins are serious or are they just playing around with him. He then decides to quickly tuck his shirt back into his pants, straighten his suit jacket and then adjust his erection.

Prancer and Vixen giggle.

Mr. Heat steps lively and opens the stall door. He closes the door after entering the stall.

Prancer looks at the small bulge in Mr. Heat's pants. "You think you can fuck…"

As if to know what her sister was going to say next, Vixen finishes Prancer's question. "…the both of us with that little thing, little man?" Vixen points to Mr. Heat's small bulge and giggles.

Prancer joins in on her sister's giggling.

Angered at the sisters' remark, Mr. Heat's face turns as red as his hair. His forehead turns into a road map of wrinkles. A large vein in his forehead starts to throb.

Mr. Heat sticks up both of his pudgy middle fingers and hollers at the twins through his tightly clenched teeth. "FUCK YOU AND FUCK YOU! I CAN FUCK THE BOTH OF YOU AND THEN SOME!"

Vixen licks both her index finger and middle finger. "Mmm… Little man has some spunk. You want to fuck my pussy first?" Vixen runs the two fingers that she licked, along her crotch.

Prancer turns her back to Mr. Heat, bends over and sticks her bare pale ass in the air. She then slaps her ass. "Or do you prefer to stick your little stiffy into my ass?" Prancer asks with a smile.

Light gray smoke rises from Mr. Heat's ears and nose.

Prancer smiles. "Oh wait, he doesn't like to fuck."

Vixen smiles. "He just likes to watch."

The twins giggle.

Prancer stands up and affectionately hugs her sister from behind while resting her chin on Vixen's shoulder. Prancer then holds her thumb and index finger about an inch apart while looking at Mr. Heat.

This causes the twins to giggle once more.

Mr. Heat screams at the twins. "FUCK THE BOTH OF YOU BITCHES!" The twins' taunting words anger Mr. Heat even more.

"Oh, look at that…" Prancer say sarcastically.

"…the wee little man is getting angry." Vixen

finishes.

The twins do as they always do when they find humor in something, they giggle.

Mr. Heat has finally had enough of the twins' taunting words. He charges Prancer and Vixen and before any one of them can do anything to defend themselves, Mr. Heat backhands Vixen so hard across the side of her face that she is thrown back against the stall then drops to her knees, holding the side of her face where she was struck.

Mr. Heat turns his anger on Prancer and grabs a handful of her hair and yanks Prancer's head back so hard that she stumbles backwards then lands on her knees.

Mr. Heat slams a tightly closed fist into Prancer's right eye several times.

Prancer whines and whimpers as she claws and grabs for Mr. Heat. She scratches at his neck, hands, and face.

Mr. Heat beats Prancer until she is unconscious. "YOU FUCKING CUNT! NO ONE SCRATCHES ME!" Mr. Heat is bleeding from the scratches on his neck, hands, and face.

Prancer's face is already red and swollen from Mr. Heat's beating. She has a cut under her right eye that is bleeding profusely. Prancer is also bleeding from her nose and mouth.

As Mr. Heat tightens the grip on Prancer's hair, his hand starts to turn a bright reddish orange color. Smoke rises from his clenched hand.

Prancer's hair starts to singe from the heat of Mr. Heat's hand.

With a push of her head, Mr. Heat let's go of Prancer's burning hair. Prancer falls into the hay that's lining the floor of the stall.

Sparks from Prancer's singed hair ignites the dry hay around her.

Mr. Heat starts to undo his pants. "I'm going to enjoy fucking that pale pussy of yours. I'm going to stick my dick so far up into you that I'm going to touch your fucking soul, you bitch."

"PRANCER!" Vixen hollers as she dives onto an unconscious Prancer while trying to frantically put out prancer's smoldering hair and the hay fire around them.

A black tan rabbit hisses as it leaps into the air, right at Mr. Heat, from one of the adjoining stalls. The black tan rabbit shapeshifts into Twiggy, in mid-air. "YOU'LL DO NO SUCH THING, YOU FUCKING PIECE OF SHIT!" Twiggy hollers to Mr. Heat as she flies through the air, towards Mr. Heat.

Twiggy lands on Mr. Heat's back, wrapping her legs around his thick body as best as she can. Twiggy then puts Mr. Heat's head into a choke hold with one arm and begins to punch him in his face from behind with her other hand. "TAKE THAT, YOU FUCKING FAT BASTARD!"

"WHAT THE FUCK!" Mr. Heat says as he turns around several times, trying to shake Twiggy off his back.

It doesn't work though because Twiggy sticks to Mr. Heat like glue while still punching him in the face.

Vixen has managed to put out Prancer's singed hair and is now sitting in the opposite corner of the stall, comforting her bruised, battered, and unconscious sister.

The hay in the corner of the stall where Prancer first fell, is now burning.

Mr. Heat slams Twiggy's back into the wrought iron grills of the stall door. "GET THE FUCK OFF ME, BITCH!"

Twiggy squeals in pain.

Mr. Heat's body temperature rises to the point where his flesh is too hot to even touch. It's almost as if his skin is on fire.

Twiggy grinds her teeth as she releases her choke

hold around Mr. Heat's neck. "OUCH!"

Mr. Heat seizes the opportunity given to him and quickly grabs the wrist of Twiggy's hand that was hitting him and with a grunt and a turn of his hips, Mr. Heat flips Twiggy off his back.

Twiggy is thrown through the air and hits the side of the stall that's on fire with such force that she smashes through the stall as if the stall was made of flimsy balsa wood.

Hot embers and burning hay fly everywhere.

Meanwhile.

An old and tired Holly Kringle has turned down the lights in her late husband's study and she is now sitting in his large, well-used, red, and green velvet armchair.

The armchair is positioned in front of an oversized stone fireplace, a fireplace that is large enough that someone can actually walk into its firebox opening.

A soft, warm glow given off by the fire in the fireplace is casting shadows across paintings of the previous owners of Christmas Village, including Holly's late husband whose painting is hung over the fireplace mantle.

Holly watches the shadows dance across the paintings as she holds an old and faded envelope in her slightly trembling hand.

Holly looks down at the envelope in her hand. She turns the envelope around and reads the name on the front of it. "To Santa Claus"

Holly looks at the envelope for a moment then opens it and takes out a neatly folded letter that's just as old and faded as the envelope that it was in.

Holly tosses the envelope into the crackling fireplace. The envelope instantly goes up in flames.

Holly carefully unfolds the old letter and begins to

read it.

Dear Santa,
 I don't want much this year Santa. Just a pistol and some caps and some firecrackers. Oh yes, and some candy would be nice. I love candy.
 Benjamin Fergus

"Auh yes, Benjamin Fergus. I remember you. You found such great joy in the presents given to you one Christmas morning." Holly thinks back many years.

Christmas morning.
4th floor of an apartment complex on East 100th Street, Manhattan.
All is quiet in the Fergus household.
Dad is nowhere to be found and hasn't made an appearance in years.
Mom, a woman with special abilities, has yet to come home from her night job.
An excited seven-year-old boy named Benjamin throws his dirty, sweaty blanket off him then jumps out of his bed and runs out to the living room where his drawing of a Christmas tree is hanging on the wall.
Benjamin's mom had told him they were broke and didn't have the money to spend on something as ridiculous as a Christmas tree and decorations. So, Benjamin found an old dirty napkin on the sidewalk and drew a Christmas tree on it. When Benjamin was done drawing his Christmas tree, he taped it to a wall.
Under his Christmas tree, on the floor, Benjamin finds four neatly wrapped presents, all with his name on them.
Benjamin starts to unwrap his gifts one after another, like a wild beast tearing into its food.

Soon, there is torn wrapping paper lying all over the place. After about fifteen minutes of running around his apartment, shooting off all his caps and eating his candy, Benjamin is out of caps for his toy pistol and all his candy is gone.

Benjamin's pistol is no longer any fun. A dust cloud rises and surrounds Benjamin as he falls back onto an old dirty, dilapidated couch that his mom got off the street.

Benjamin picks up his firecrackers off the couch and looks at them, wondering what kind of fun he can have with them. After a few minutes of thinking to himself, Benjamin gets an idea after he hears the neighbor's cat, Mr. Sneezer in the hallway, outside of his apartment door, meowing.

Mr. Sneezer was at one time a beautiful Himalayan cat with beautiful long white fur with spots of cream-tortie coloring and a small pink nose.

Mr. Sneezer got his name from the way he purred. When he would purr, Mr. Sneezer would let out a small noise afterwards that sounded like a sneeze.

Now Mr. Sneezer's fur is heavily matted and black from years of neglect. Hundreds of fleas have also made poor Mr. Sneezer their home.

It takes Benjamin awhile to catch Mr. Sneezer but with the help of a wooden baseball bat that his mom keeps by the door, Mr. Sneezer is lying on Benjamin's bedroom floor with its head smashed to a bloody pulp.

Benjamin kneels beside Mr. Sneezer with his firecrackers, a roll of tape and his mom's lighter.

Benjamin tapes Mr. Sneezer's front legs together with some of the firecrackers and then Mr. Sneezer's back legs.

Once Benjamin is done, he picks Mr. Sneezer up by

his tail and stands up with his mom's lighter in his other hand. He walks over to a broken window that looks out over an alleyway. Benjamin sets Mr. Sneezer's lifeless body and lighter on the windowsill.

    Benjamin can smell the garbage in the alleyway, down below as a small winter breeze blows in through the broken window.

    Benjamin picks Mr. Sneezer up by his tail and then the lighter. He looks at the firecrackers taped to Mr. Sneezer's legs. Benjamin smiles as he lights the firecrackers.

    As the fuses quickly ignite, Benjamin throws Mr. Sneezer's body out the broken window and into the alleyway.

    Halfway down, the firecrackers explode. "BANG! BANG! BANG! BANG! BANG! BANG!"

    Back to the present time.

    "You then went on to become a career criminal and then take up permanent residence at your local gray bar hotel where you eventually died of tuberculosis. I told papa those weren't suitable toys for a child your age but being who he was, papa insisted on giving you what you wanted as he did with every child." Holly sits up in her chair as she balls up Benjamin's letter and throws it into the fireplace.

    The letter is so old and brittle that as soon as the balled-up letter comes into contact with the heat from the fire, the letter disintegrates into ashes even before it touches the actual fire.

    The fire hisses and crackles.

    Holly sits back in her chair and enjoys the hypnotic movements of the fire as it dances around in the fireplace.

    There's a light knock followed by the study door creaking open.

    Eggnog pops his head in. "Excuse me mother. I

have the rest of the letters." Eggnog waits for Holly to answer before he walks into the study any further.
    Holly doesn't answer.
    Eggnog clears his throat then, "Excuse me mother… the letters?" Eggnog waits again for a response.
    Holly still doesn't say a word. She just sticks an arm out from around the chair and motions for Eggnog to come in.
    Eggnog pushes open the door and walks in, dragging a large, overly stuffed, red velvet bag behind him.
    Eggnog doesn't get no more than a few feet into the study when Cupid bursts in, almost knocking over Eggnog.
    "HEY! WHAT THE HELL IS THE BIG IDEA!" Eggnog hollers to Cupid. He then drops the overly stuffed bag, allowing for some of the letters to fall out.
    Cupid ignores Eggnog and hollers to Holly. "HE'S AT IT AGAIN MOTHER! MR. HEAT AND THE TWINS ARE FIGHTING IN THE BARN!"
    "THAT MOTHERFUCKER!" Holly leaps out of her chair and bolts past Cupid and Eggnog.

    A few minutes later.
    Ever since the sickness, the barn has been quiet and somewhat peaceful but when an enraged Holly whips open the barn door, just about taking it off its hinges, she is greeted with chaos throughout the whole barn.
    Holly is still in her older form. "WHERE IS THAT LITTLE FUCKER!"
    There is a large plume of gray smoke rising to the upper rafters of the barn.
    Cupid and Eggnog hurry in behind Holly.
    Holly quickly scans the barn. She sees Nester in his stall, kicking it, trying to get out while braying loudly. "HEE-HAW! HEE-HAW! HEE-HAW!"
    The walls of Nester's stall crack from his kicks but

they do not give way.

Cupid rushes to Nester's stall to calm him down before he hurts himself.

Holly then looks to her left and sees Snowman in Vixen's stall, putting out a fire with snow shooting out from his own body.

Snow is shooting out from Snowman's mid-section like a snowblower shooting out snow. The snow coming from Snowman is creating a mini snowstorm in Vixen's stall and part of the stall that Twiggy crashed through.

Vixen and Prancer are on the outside of Vixen's stall, sitting down. Vixen is comforting Prancer in her arms while patting Prancer's hair, trying to put out any remaining sparks that have singed Prancer's hair.

It is too late though. The damage to Prancer's hair has been done. Her beautiful platinum blond hair is no more. All that is left is a head full of singed hair.

Eggnog runs over to Vixen's stall and looks in. He then looks over to the adjoining stall where Twiggy was thrown through. "TWIGGY!" Eggnog hollers as he notices Twiggy lying in the stall, unconscious.

Eggnog whips open the stall door that Twiggy is in and rushes to her side.

When Holly doesn't see Mr. Heat, she runs out of the barn.

A thick and heavy snowstorm is making it hard to see anything. It continues to get worse by the minute.

Mr. Heat is hurrying down one of Christmas Village's many snow covered paths. Or at least Mr. Heat thinks he is on a path. He can't really tell with all the snow coming down.

To keep himself warm from the harsh weather, Mr. Heat magically raises his body temperature. His body now has a slight reddish orange glow to it while his hair looks as if it's on fire.

Mr. Heat stuffs his hands into the pockets of his suite pants and mumbles to himself as he continues to make his way through the snow.

Then, a familiar sound makes Mr. Heat stop dead in his tracks. It is a noise he knows all too well.

Mr. Heat hears a soft drawn-out whistle coming from somewhere in the snowstorm. He quickly takes his hands out of his pockets and slowly turns around. He knows who is whistling but he still squints as hard as he can to see through the thick snow.

The whistling stops and is then followed by a dark silhouette of someone walking towards Mr. Heat, through the thick snowstorm.

Just like the whistling, the snowstorm stops abruptly, leaving behind large mounds of snow everywhere, as far as the eye can see.

An angry, old, timeworn Holly stands in front of Mr. Heat. She doesn't say a word.

"Let me guess, one of the prickteasers went crying to mommy." Mr. Heat says sarcastically then puts his hands in the air to simulate a small explosion. "And… POOF! Mommy is here to save the day." Mr. Heat puts his hands down and waits for Holly to say something in response to his actions.

Holly just stands in front of Mr. Heat, not saying a word.

She never did like the little fucker. It was Holly's husband that got along with him. But now that her husband is gone, it would bring Holly so much pleasure to snuff out this hot head son of a bitch. All she has to do is freeze the air around his head until he suffocates from lack of oxygen.

Holly breaks her silence. "I never did like you. I should have left your crusty ass in that asylum to rot."

Taken back by what Holly has just told him, "Well

damn, I didn't know we were having confession. Shit, I better confess my sins then."

Already furious at Mr. Heat, Holly bites her bottom lip to keep herself from saying anything.

Mr. Heat clears his throat with an evil mischievous smile. "Do you remember that little red nosed bitch?" Mr. Heat asks then waits for an answer, an answer that never comes.

Holly crosses her arms in front of her as her wrinkly face gets hard and ridged. She has an idea of where Mr. Heat is going with his question.

Mr. Heat notices the reaction on Holly's face. "Oh... You do remember that whiney fucking bitch." Mr. Heat takes a step or two away from Holly as he looks down while kicking some snow. He then looks up at Holly who is still staring at him.

If looks could kill, Mr. Heat would be dead where he stands.

Mr. Heat clears his throat once more. "One winter night when everyone had finished playing their reindeer games and they were tucked in their beds, fast asleep, I got the case of the munchies. When I couldn't find anything that I liked in the kitchen, I went out to the barn and lured that red nosed bitch far away from her parents where I in return, gutted and skinned her little body. I then gorged myself on her tender, juicy meat. It melted in my mouth just like butter. When I was done, all that was left was her cleaned bones." Mr. Heat moans and licks his lips. "That was the best meal that I had in a long time."

Holly has had enough. She balls up her fist and lunges at Mr. heat. "YOU DIRTY SON OF A..."

Mr. Heat quickly steps away from Holly as he puts his hands up to stop Holly before she makes contact with him.

"WAITE!... WAITE!... WAITE!... Heres' the best

part." Mr. Heat smiles from ear to ear. "Do you know, if you cook the nose of a reindeer calf just right, it's like eating a delicious gummy bear that's loaded with so much flavor that when you bite down on it, it explodes in your mouth. But with a nose as red and bright as that little bitch had, I put the whole fucker in my mouth. And when I sunk my teeth into it, it was like eating a warm maraschino cherry but with the chewy consistency of a gummy bear." Mr. Heat closes his eye and smacks his lips. "Oh, it was delicious." Mr. Heat then opens his eyes and looks at Holly. "Oh, and I bet you didn't know, your fat, lard ass husband found out what I had done. He didn't have it in him to kill me so, he had me locked away in that asylum until you busted me out."

A single tear rolls down Holly's cheek. She then takes her turn to do the talking.

As Holly looks at the scratches on Mr. Heat's face, neck and hands, "Do you remember what I said I was going to have done to you if you ever put another hand on my family?" Holly calmly asks Mr. Heat.

Mr. Heat doubles over with laughter then, "You're not going to do a fucking thing to me you fucking cunt."

Holly clenches her fists tight as her face turns beet red. She bites down on her bottom lip again.

It's taking every ounce of willpower that Holly has to keep her from lunging at Mr. Heat.

Mr. Heat puts his hands together in front of him as he notices that Holly isn't too happy with his choice words. "Oh, did I hit a nerve?" Mr. Heat pauses for a second then, "Or is it that you're just an old decrepit piece of shit that just realized, you can't do squat to me, let alone rip my head…" Mr. Heat stops before he finishes what he is saying and smells the cold winter air.

It's then that Mr. Heat realizes the error he has made in assuming that the feeble old woman standing in

front of him was the one who was going to rip his head off.
 Frostbite steps out of a huge snowbank and into the open. He stands, towering over Mr. Heat. Snow falls from Frostbite's massive body as he growls and snorts at Mr. Heat.
 Before Mr. Heat can turn around, Frostbite snatches him up by his neck with one hand while at the same time, putting his other massive hand over Mr. Heat's face and squeezes.
 Mr. Heat kicks and screams as he lashes out at Frostbite's hands that are around his face and neck.
 Frostbite's fingernails dig into Mr. Heat's face. Frostbite then pulls on Mr. Heat's head and body in opposite directions.
 Mr. Heat stops his kicking and screaming as his head is ripped from his plump little body.
 Frostbite let's out a loud satisfying growl that echoes throughout Christmas Village.
 Blood from Mr. Heat's head and body flies everywhere. Mr. Heat's blood is like lava and melts the snow that it touches.
 Some of Frostbite's fur is singed but other than that, Frostbite is unaffected by the hot temperature of Mr. Heat's blood.
 Frostbite lets Mr. Heat's head fly off into a snowbank, behind him. He then throws Mr. Heat's bleeding, lifeless body into the snow, between him and Holly.
 Frostbite's head and upper body are covered and stained with Mr. Heat's blood.
 Blood gushing out of Mr. Heat's headless body melts the snow around it.
 Holly lifts her dress out of the snow and carefully steps over Mr. Heat's lifeless body, being careful to not let her dress touch any of Mr. Heat's blood.

As she straddles his lifeless body, Holly looks down at Mr. Heat's bleeding, headless body. "I told you I was going to piss down your neck." Holly looks up at the sky, closes her eyes and lets out a sigh of relief as she pisses on Mr. Heat.

As soon as Holly and Frostbite are out of site, Pepper steps out from behind a snowbank where she had been hiding with small glass vials. Pepper bends down beside Mr. Heat's decapitated body, being ever so careful as to not get any of Mr. Heat's blood on her. Pepper then fills her vials with Mr. Heat's blood.

12

TRAILER PARK TRASH

Twin Lakes Trailer Park, Upstate, New York.
All is quiet in Twin Lakes Trailer Park.
The residence of Twin Lakes have settled in for the night. Their bellies are full from dinner and now most of them are either enjoying some family time or watching TV. Some have even gone to bed.
And then you have… Dorothy Hand, a three hundred and twenty-five-pound mother of two little girls. Dorothy has been left alone to care for her children while her husband, Richard, takes part in a big game hunting expedition in Africa.
A small figure stands in the shadows, peering into one of the windows of the Hand double wide mobile home. The figure watches and listens as Dorothy threatens her children.
Dorothy threatens her little girls with hateful words. "YOU LITTLE FUCKING BASTARDS! STOP YOUR GOD DAMN FIGHTING OR I'M GOING TO BEAT YOUR ASSES RAW!"
The shadowed figure can't see the kids, but the figure can hear them.
"SHE STARTED IT!" Screams one of the girls.
Then the other girl. "NO, SHE DID!"

The shadowed figure still cannot see the girls, but she does see an extremely large Dorothy with her back turned towards her.

Dorothy raises a big meaty hand high into the air. "I told the both of you to stop your fucking fighting." Dorothy quicky brings her open hand down and makes contact with one of the little girls' asses.

The shadowed figure cannot see who Dorothy had struck. But whomever Dorothy struck, it made a loud slapping sound.

There's a loud scream followed by crying and whimpering from the little girl that was slapped.

Dorothy raises her hand again. "YOU BETTER NOT CRY!" and once more she brings her meaty hand down hard. "AND YOU SURE AS HELL BETTER NOT POUT!"

The shadowed figure disappears into the cold night.

From inside the mobile home, Dorothy is heard hollering at her kids. "NOW GET TO BED BEFORE I BEAT YOUR FUCKING ASSES!"

A few minutes later, Dorothy steps out of her modest, double wide mobile home with a cigarette hanging out of her mouth.

Because of her weight and size, the mobile home slightly rocks as Dorothy steps down into an enclosed metal carport.

With a face like Frankenstein's monster, you'd think she was a guy. Her somewhat of a flat head covered with greasy brown hair, big forehead and square jaw. Dorothy's nose has such an arch to it that it looks like it has been broke many times. Her thick bushy eyebrows are missing a few hairs to make it a full unibrow. The dark peach fuzz on her upper lip is just as bad.

The only think that distinguishes Dorothy from a man are her large breasts but then again, they could more of her many rolls.

Dorothy is wearing a pink flannel robe with matching pants and pink fuzzy slippers.

Dorothy lets the mobile home door slam behind her. She walks to the back of the carport while taking a drag on her cigarette until there's only the butt of the cigarette left. Dorothy then flicks the lit cigarette on the ground as she exhales, letting the cigarette smoke roll out of her mouth and nose.

Dorothy mutters under her breath. "Those fucking bastards. Whatever the fuck possessed me to have kids, beats the fuck out of me. I should have had my fucking head examined."

With her back to the opened entrance of the carport, Dorothy puts another cigarette between her yellow, extremely gappy teeth, lights it and puffs away like a chimney. She closes her eyes and welcomes the sounds of the trailer park.

A few cars can be heard honking their horns as they drive by on the other side of the trailer park. Dorothy can also hear the muffled sound of a neighbor's T.V.

The sound of snow crunch as if someone is walking in it, is getting closer to Dorothy's carport.

A gentle cold breeze blows in a slight aroma of peppermint candy canes through the carport's entrance and brings in some of the falling snow with it.

Dorothy drops her unfinished cigarette on the ground and puts it out with the bottom of a pink fuzzy slipper.

The shadowed figure that was standing outside of Dorothy's window a few minutes ago steps into view at the carport's opened entrance with a large red velvet sack slung over her shoulder. "Holy shit, look at the girth on you. No wonder you live in a double wide."

Dorothy quickly turns around with a surprised

expression. "Excuse me?" She asks.

Standing in the carport's entrance is a five-foot-tall woman whose head and face are hidden by an oversized hood. Tufts of red hair are blowing out from under the woman's hood.

The woman is wearing an oversized hooded parka overcoat with a stitched burgundy and white patchwork pattern. The coat also has large white fur trim around the hood, zipper area, wrists and on the inside of the coat. The coat is also hiding most of the woman's red and white candy cane striped mini dress.

The woman's candy cane decorated knee high white fur leg warmers and pom-pom ties match her mini dress.

The woman slowly pulls the hood off her head. She is sucking on a red and white striped candy cane.

The woman takes the candy cane out of her mouth. The end of the candy cane has been sucked to a point. "Oh dear. Now that's not nice to say about your children. It's not the children's fault they are the way they are." The woman pauses for a second then, "You know, I blame the children's actions and up brining on their parents or guardian."

"And who the fuck are you?" Dorothy asks as she takes a step towards the woman.

The woman introduces herself. "My friends call me Pepper, but you can call me, Peppermint, you fucked up trailer park trash. You have something mother wants, and she has sent me to collect it." Pepper can feel the hairs on her body stand on end.

Dorothy's face turns beet red. As she gets angrier, Dorothy's eyebrows come together to form a unibrow. "Excuse me? What did you just say?"

Pepper looks to her right then to her left. She then looks at Dorothy with a puzzled expression. "Did I studder, you fat sow?"

Dorothy balls up a fist and cocks it back as she takes a few more steps towards Pepper. "Why you skinny ass bitch. I don't know who the fuck you are, but you better get the fuck off my property before I shove my fucking hand up your ass."

Pepper notices four little round eyes peering out at her from behind some drawn curtains from inside Dorothy's mobile home. The eyes are glossy and bloodshot.

Pepper smiles and waves.

Dorothy also notices the four little eyes looking out and recognizes them as belonging to her two little girls. "GET THE FUCK TO BED BEFORE I BEAT YOUR FUCKING ASSES AGAIN!"

The four little eyes quickly disappear.

Pepper slowly turns to Dorothy. The corners of Pepper's mouth curl upwards as a mischievous smile washes over Pepper's face. "You may get away with threatening and beating your kids but that won't work too well with me, I guarantee you that."

"Oh, that's it, you fucking bitch." Dorothy charges Pepper as fast as her overweight body will allow her to go. She clenches her meaty hands closed, ready to strike.

When Dorothy reaches Pepper, she attempts to swing at Pepper's head but misses when Pepper ducks out of the way.

Pepper quickly stands up and thrusts her candy cane, point first, deep into Dorothy's nose until only the warble is sticking out.

Dorothy stands up straight. Her eyes roll to the back of her head. Blood runs out of Dorothy's candy cane filled nostril.

Pepper giggles as she admires her handy work.

Dorothy teeters back and forth.

Pepper takes a deep breath then blows up at

Dorothy's face.
    Dorothy falls back, flat on her back.

    A few minutes have passed as Pepper is now struggling to fit Dorothy's sizeable dead body into her sack. Dorothy is just as big around as the sack's opening.
    With just Dorothy's feet sticking out, Pepper gives her sack a yank or two and after some grunts and groans, Dorothy is finally inside Pepper's sack.
    Pepper sinches the velvet sack closed and stands up. She slings the sack over her shoulder as if it were just a sack of feathers.
    Pepper turns to the mobile home and whispers.
"Now for the little ones."

13

A TRUE APEX PREDATORE

A small charter plane carrying four men and one woman, touches down on a small dirt airstrip in Zimbabwe. As the plane reaches the end of the runway, it circles around to face the way it came from and then stops.

Two filthy, open-sided 4x4 land rovers drive out onto the airstrip. The land rovers stop alongside the plane.

The passenger doors of the land rovers open and out steps four men wearing khaki pants, olive green t-shirts and tan camouflage jackets.

The four men welcome the passengers of the charter plane as they disembark.

The first passenger off the plane is a tall, slender, sixty year old man, carrying a duffle bag. The man is wearing a Stuart Hughes Diamond Edition suite. His name is Dr. Eugene Masters, a plastic surgeon from Beverly Hills.

Next out of the plane is Jimmy Jacobs, a plump and round faced sandwich shop owner from Illinois. His baseball cap is on backwards, exposing his large sweaty forehead. Jimmy's Polo shirt is unbuttoned half way down his hairy chest so he can air out his sweat drenched, hairy chest.

Jimmy takes out a handkerchief from his back

pocket and dabs the beads of sweat from his forehead. He then returns the now damp handkerchief to his back pocket and shakes the hands of his hosts.

A tall, blond-haired woman is the next to get off the small plane. She brushes away a few strands of hair from her face as she introduces herself to the men that got out of the land rovers. "Hello, I'm Rebecca Dickerson." She shakes each one of the men's hands.

Finally… Richard Hand and Edward Long are the last two passengers off the plane.

Three of the four men that got out of the land rovers retrieve everyone's luggage while the fourth man address the people that just got off the plane. He has got a strong African accent. "Hello, my name is Bahati, and I'll be your guide for the duration of your expedition. Now, if all of you would get into the vehicles, we'll take you back to camp for some food, a change of clothes and then we'll get you started on your expedition." The guide motions to the two land rovers.

Richard, Edward, and Rebecca get into one land rover while Dr. Masters and Jimmy get into the second land rover.

When everyone is in the land rovers, the land rovers speed off.

Sometime later.

Bellies have been stuffed, the appropriate clothing has been put on and now the hunt has begun.

Richard and Bahati are lying in some tall grass, downwind of a pride of lions while the rest of the hunting party watches from the safety of their land rover which is only one hundred yards away.

Richard sets his sights on the oldest and biggest of the two male lions of the pride.

The lion that Richard is watching is basking in the

sun while the rest of the pride is either sleeping or grooming themselves. The pride's six cubs are making a game out of chasing each other.

The pride is unaware their protector is about to be taken from them by their only real natural enemy… man.

Richard takes a slow, deep breath and as he exhales, squeezing the trigger, something startles the pride.

The pride quickly jumps to their feet.

An explosion echoes throughout the grasslands.

As quickly as the protector of the pride rises, he soon drops to the ground where he was just lying down.

Startled, the rest of the pride run off, leaving their fallen leader behind.

After Bahati and his men have made sure the pride in nowhere to be found, Richard is then allowed to admire his kill.

Before the dead lion is loaded into the back of the land rover, Richard hands Edward his phone. "Here, buddy. Do you mind taking my picture? I want to show Dorothy and the kids what I'm bringing home."

Edward takes Richard's phone. "Sure. Strike a pose."

Richard straddles the dead lion and does a double bicep pose while clenching his teeth. Richard grunts as Edward takes the picture.

Edward hands Richard his phone.

Richard looks at the picture that Edward took then, "Wait, hold on. Just one more."

Edward sighs then shakes his head as he smiles at Richard. "Alright, come on. These guys want to load up the lion and get out of here before the pride returns."

Richard sits on the lion's back and lifts the lion's massive head so they are cheek to cheek.

Richard can smell the musky odor coming from the lion's fur. The rank stench coming from the lion's mouth isn't any better.

While holding the lion's head up, Richard clenches his teeth and growls.

Edward takes the picture of Richard and the lion.

The next day continues with Dr. Masters' hunt.

Dr. Masters and Bahati are tracking down a herd of cape buffalo also known as the black death, at a watering hole.

Dr. Masters uses some tall brush for cover as he and Bahati watch the herd drink from the watering hole.

There are also zebras and impalas drinking from the same watering hole.

Dr, Masters watches and waits in silence until he spots the one cape buffalo that he has come to Africa for. The largest of the herd, a one thousand, nine-hundred-and-ten-pound bull with horns that span forty inches across with a broad thick shield.

Bahati quietly taps Dr. Masters on his should then points to the herd around the bull.

The bull continues to drink from the watering hole as the rest of the herd starts to move away from the watering hole.

A few zebras and impalas remain at the watering hole with the bull.

As Dr. Masters carefully shifts his weight, an impala lifts its head up from the watering hole and looks around.

Dr. Masters and Bahati freeze where they are then wait until the impala goes back to drinking from the watering hole.

Dr. Masters lifts his rifle up and points it at the bull. He looks down the barrel of his rifle and spots his prize. He takes a deep breath and pulls the trigger.

The loud bang from Dr. Masters' rifle causes the

animals around the watering hole to take off running.

The only animal that doesn't run is the large cape buffalo bull. Instead, the cape buffalo bull drops like a lead weight.

Dr. Masters turns to Bahati with a childish smile and giggles. "The black death?... I don't think so." Dr. Masters turns back to the fallen bull. "His head is going to look amazing above my office chair."

Later that day.

Four of the five hunters are in the back seat of a land rover with two guides in the front seat. The four hunters are looking through binoculars, out onto the grasslands.

Up on the rooftop of the land rover is Rebecca. She is lying on her belly with an elephant gun in hand.

It is Rebecca's turn to claim her prize and she has found it. A lone thirteen-thousand-pound bull elephant, standing ten feet tall and six feet in length.

Rebecca didn't come all this way for the elephant's hide or its meat. Instead, Rebecca has come for the elephant's magnificent ivory tusks.

Seeing the bull elephant in all his glory, excites Rebecca so much that she starts to drool profusely.

Rebecca puts the elephant gun down and takes her eyes off the bull elephant so she can wipe the drool off her mouth with her sleeve.

Rebecca hears shouting inside the land rover. She then looks up.

There, standing in the clearing is the bull elephant that Rebecca was watching. The bull elephant is now watching Rebecca. It flaps its ears back and forth and shaking its head while making loud trumpeting sounds.

"COME ON, SHOOT THE FUCKER! SHOOT HIM!" The other hunters holler to Rebecca from in the land rover.

Rebecca angrily slaps the roof of the land rover.
"SHUT THE FUCK UP BEFORE YOU SCARE HIM OFF!" Rebecca lines up the barrel of her elephant gun with the bull elephant's forehead.

"What the fuck are you waiting for? Christmas? Take your shot." Jimmy asks Rebecca through an open window.

The elephant takes a few steps towards the land rover.

There is such a sudden chill on top of the land rover that Rebecca can see her own breath.

As Rebecca slowly pulls back on the trigger of her gun, an invisible finger taps Rebecca on her shoulder.

Startled, Rebecca quickly looks behind her to see who's on the rooftop with her. But when she turns around, there is no one there.

The temperature inside the land rover drops as ice crystals start to form on the inside of the land rover's windows.

Everyone in the land rover is surprised at the temperature drop. Cold temperatures like this are something unheard of in Africa.

A few of the men try to clear the windows of the ice crystals so they can see out the windows.

The driver of the land rover starts the engine.

Rebecca quickly turns back around and takes aim at the elephant.

The bull elephant charges the land rover.

As the land rover backs up, an explosion is heard coming from the rooftop of the land rover. Seconds later, the bull elephant collapses.

The men inside the land rover hear Rebecca's elephant gun go off. They look out a part of the windshield that hasn't been covered in ice crystals. The men watch as

the bull elephant falls to the ground.
A huge dust cloud envelopes the fallen elephant.

Sometime has passed since Rebecca dropped the elephant.
Rebecca is sitting on the ground with her back resting on the belly of the dead elephant. The elephant's tusks have been cut off and are now on the ground, beside Rebecca.
Rebecca fluffs the elephant's belly as if it were a pillow. She then crosses her legs and clasps her fingers behind her head. Rebecca sighs. "I love my life." Rebecca closes her eyes. "It can't get any better than this."
One of the guides stands on the hood of the land rover and takes a picture of Rebecca as she enjoys her kill.

Later that night, bellies have been stuffed, stories have been exchanged. Now everyone is in bed sleeping for the night, except for Richard who is lying on his cot, staring at the ceiling.
The buzzing and clicking of the cicadas outside of the hut was lolling Richard to sleep but now that Edward's chainsaw snoring has gotten so loud, Richard cannot sleep.
Richard grunts then wraps his pillow around his head so that it covers both of his ears.
If Edward's snoring were any louder, someone would think a pride of lions were roaring in Richard and Edward's hut.
The pillow over Richard's ears doesn't help one bit. Richard can still hear Edward's snoring as if he were doing it right in his ear.
Having enough, Richard sits up in bed. "What the hell. Wake the fuck up Edward." Richard throws his pillow at Edward. "No wonder Nancy has you sleep on the couch."

Edward mumbles in his sleep then turns onto his side.

Richard is wide awake now. He decides to get up and get some fresh air and even some peace and quiet.

The hut is pitch dark. So, without any source of light, Richard carefully makes his way through the dark hut until he comes to what he thinks is the door to the hut.

It's apparent that a big cat has been through the camp or at least the surrounding area, marking its territory because as Richard steps outside, he smells what seems to be hot buttered popcorn.

The popcorn odor is so strong that if you were to close your eyes, you'd think you were at the concession stand of a movie theater.

There is also a strong pungent odor that alerts Richard of elephants being in the area as well.

Richard looks up at the night sky and sees a shooting star dance across the sky.

He then closes his eyes and stretches his arms out to his side. "Oh yes, the great outdoors." Richard says as he takes in the popcorn and the pungent smell of the elephants.

There is a sudden chill in the air.

Richard quickly rubs both of his arms to get warm. "Where in the hell did that come?" Richard refers to the chill.

Richard also notices, the cicadas have stopped their singing. The distant sound of lions roaring has also stopped.

As a matter of fact, everything in the African grasslands has gone eerily silent.

Richard has got goose bumps on both of his arms and the hairs on the back of his neck is standing on end.

As Richard starts to slowly back up into his hut, something else unheard of in the African grasslands starts to happen. A light snowfall starts coming down.

"What the fuck." Surprised, Richard turns back around to the entrance of his hut. He opens the door and hollers for Edward. "EDWARD, GET YOUR ASS OUT HERE AND TAKE A LOOK AT THIS SHIT! EDWARD!"

Richard continues to watch the snow come down. Edward eventually walks out of the hut, wearing just a pair of boxers.

Still drowsy, Edward rubs his eyes. "What the fuck is the big idea of waking me up?"

Richard doesn't say a word, he just watches in awe as the snow continues to blanket the African grasslands.

Edward now notices the snow. "What the hell. Where'd this shit come from?"

Everyone else has now woken up and standing outside their hut, still half asleep and wondering why they've been woken up in the middle of the night. A few of them are rubbing their arms trying to get warm.

Jimmy is standing in the doorway of his hut with just a pair of white boxers on with his fat, round, tattooed belly hanging out.

The silence is broken by the sound of a loud, raspy cough that sounds like someone trying to saw through a tree.

Then, out of the darkness, five leopards slowly and stealthily slink their way towards the hunting party. The leopards' heads are low with their legs bent, ready to strike.

The leopards do not seem to be bothered by the snow.

The hunting party hears a mix of low-pitched roars and medium-pitched roars. Then, a pride of lions consisting of four males and twelve lionesses with cubs in tow walk into view, not far behind the leopards.

The hunting party is surprised at what they see.

"WHAT THE FUCK!" Dr. Masters says with a

shocked expression.

"HOLY SHIT!" Edward says as he quickly retreats to his hut for his gun.

A few of the other hunters follow suit.

As the hunters return with their rifles in hand, they are surprised to see cape buffalo, rhinos and elephants have now joined the lions and leopards.

At first, the hunting party stands gawking at the animals. Then as the animals get closer, the ones who retrieved their rifles take aim.

The animals stop advancing towards the hunters. They also stop their growling and roaring, as if someone had told them to be quiet.

For a few seconds, there is silence.

The hunters look at each other with puzzled expressions, wondering why the animals stopped.

A soft, drawn out whistle breaks the silence.

The snow stops coming down except for a six-foot snow devil that appears from out of nowhere, between two elephants.

"I wouldn't do that if I were you." A female voice cautions the hunters.

A young Holly steps out of the snow devil wearing her powder blue velvet dress. The hood attached to Holly's capelet has been pulled over her head, hiding her face.

Just as Holly steps all the way out of the snow devil, Jimmy is hit on the back of his head, knocking him unconscious.

Jimmy eventually wakes up with an excruciating headache.

Jimmy and the rest of the hunting party are lined up outside of their huts, seated and tied to chairs that have been brought out from inside the huts.

All the animals are gathered around in a large circle,

around the five hunters and six guides.

Jimmy looks around with a painful but confused look on his face. "What the hell." Jimmy says to himself.

The snow devil has disappeared and in its place is Holly and Eggnog who are standing side by side.

Jimmy uses a loud and threatening tone as he screams to Holly. "WHO THE FUCK ARE YOU, BITCH!"

The guides and the rest of the hunting party are not as brave as Jimmy. They instead, remain silent and petrified with fear.

Holly and Eggnog look at each other with evil smiles. They then take a few steps towards Jimmy.

"It seems that you and your friends have made the naughty list this year, Mr. Jacobs." Holly says with a smile.

"WHAT THE FUCK DO YOU MEAN, NAUGHTY LIST?" Jimmy hollers to Holly again as he struggles with his binds.

Prancer and Vixen step out of the darkness, behind Jimmy, wearing their full length, white gothic trench coats and their white leather, high platform boots.

The twins have also cut their platinum blond hair. They both have matching pixie cuts with just a slight variation to Vixen's. The sides of Vixen's head have been shaven.

Most of the bruising around Prancer's eyes from the beating that Mr. Heat gave her is covered up by her smokey eyes but the cut under her right eye is still noticeable.

Vixen slaps the side of Jimmy's face so hard that she leaves a bright red welt mark of her hand on the side of his face.

"Santa's naughty list, of course. Duh!" The twins say in unison.

Jimmy moans in pain from the slap on his face.

The tribal tattoo on Jimmy's belly catches Eggnog's

attention.

Eggnog waddles up to Jimmy and points to Jimmy's oversized belly as he leans in closer to inspect the tattoo. The tribal tattoo is of a reindeer with large antlers and a bright red nose.

"What is this?" Eggnog asks Jimmy.

Jimmy ignores Eggnog's question.

Eggnog turns to the twins with a mischievous smile then back to the tattoo on Jimmy's belly. Eggnog inspects the tattoo a bit more before turning to the twins again.

Eggnog looks at Jimmy's tattoo once more and points to it. "That looks nothing like our little girl."

Jimmy spits a large slimy snot ball at Eggnog. "FUCK YOU!"

The snot ball misses Eggnog and hits the ground, in front of Eggnog.

Eggnog looks at the slimy snot on the ground then takes a few quick steps towards Jimmy as he balls up the gnarled fingers of one hand. He pulls his clenched fist back then lets it fly forward, into Jimmy's lower jaw.

If Jimmy hadn't been tied to his chair, he would have been knocked out of it.

Jimmy moans.

The rest of hunting party watches in fear.

Eggnog grabs onto Jimmy's jaw so that he can't move his head. Eggnog's gnarly looking fingernails dig into Jimmy's flesh.

Blood trickles down Eggnog's fingers.

Eggnog returns Jimmy's gift and spits at Jimmy. However, Eggnog doesn't miss like Jimmy did. Eggnog's saliva enters Jimmy's nostrils and mouth.

Eggnog lets go of Jimmy and gently slaps the side of Jimmy's face. Eggnog then walks to the twins and stands by them.

Jimmy gags on the saliva in his mouth then throws

up.

"Well Mr. Jacobs, you've built quite the sandwich empire off the carcasses of big game animals. Some of which are now extinct. What the fuck is wrong with you people?" Holly says as she takes a few slow steps towards Jimmy. "Hell, you even have sports athletes organizing fighting rings for dogs and pitting them against each other and doing so without remorse or asking for forgiveness. And some would call me the monster."

Unmoved by Holly's words, Jimmy threatens Holly. "FUCK YOU BITCH! When I get out of here, I'm going to add your fucking head to my trophy wall."

Prancer and Vixen look at each other with wide eyed surprised expressions.

As Holly continues to make her way to Jimmy, she motions for Eggnog to go into one of the huts.

Eggnog disappears into one of the huts.

When Holly finally reaches Jimmy, she positions herself behind him with both of her hands resting on his shoulders. "Now Mr. Jacobs, you're not going to do a damn thing to me or my family. You on the other hand are going to learn what it's like to be hunted by a true apex predator." Holly steps away from Jimmy.

Eggnog exits the hut he had walked into, with an arm full of apples and follows Holly as she walks to the other end of where the hunting guides are seated and tied.

Eggnog hands an apple to Holly.

As Holly takes the apple handed to her, "Actually, all of you are going to find out what it's like to be hunted." Holly places the apple on Bahati's head.

Bahati is trembling with fear.

Holly leans into the Bahati's ear and whispers. "Now don't move." As she stands up, "But you know what? I'm not such an evil monster. I'm going to give you a choice. Something you don't offer your prey." Holly takes another apple and places it on the head of the next guide. "And the choice is... You can either sit in these chairs and except your punishment." Holly continues to set apples on everyone's heads. "Or, when my children cut you free, you're more than welcome to get up and run from the animals that you hunt." Holly sets the last apple on Jimmy's head.

The twins untie everyone

The hunters and their guides all have looks of horror frozen on their faces. Each one wondering if they'd be fast enough to outrun the animals long enough to find safety.

Holly puts her hands in the air. "Hold on. Before you decide on what you want to do, let me explain your punishment, if I may." Holly walks behind Richard and Edward and takes the apples off their heads then tosses one of the apples to Eggnog. Holly takes a bite out of her apple before tossing it to a waiting lion who then devours it in one bite.

Holly chews the apple in her mouth then swallows it.

Eggnog eats the apple that Holly tossed to him until all that's left is the core. He then drops the core on the ground.

Holly begins to explain the punishment as she stares out into the darkness in front of her. "Two hundred and forty-nine yards out there in the darkness is an apex predator, a true apex predator like no other." Holly steps away from Edward and Richard as she lets out a soft, drawn out whistle.

Seconds after Holly stops whistling, another whistle is heard cutting through the darkness. A different whistle. A high-pitched whistle.

An arrow made of solid ice lands at the feet of Bahati.

Holly looks at the arrow stuck in the ground. "Well, I'll be. She never misses. I guess it's your lucky day." Holly tells the hunting guide who had the arrow land at his feet.

Bahati leaps out of his chair and runs into the darkness. Three other guides follow him. The apples that were on their heads fall to the ground.

A few of the lions and leopards disappear into the darkness, after the men.

Screams and roars are heard coming from the darkness where the guides ran into. The sound of flesh being ripped apart can also be heard.

The hunters and the remaining guides sit up straight in their chairs, frozen with fear.

Holly puts a hand on Richard and Edward's shoulder as she stands behind them. "And then there were seven." Holly looks at Richard then Edward. "Don't worry boys, I have other plans for you." She smiles at Richard and Edward.

The same high-pitched whistle that was heard before is heard again followed by five more arrows made of ice appear out of nowhere.

Giving the hunters and remaining guides no time to react, the arrows find their mark. Some of the arrows bury themselves in the middle of a forehead while others hit right square on the bridge of a nose.

The apples that were placed on the hunting party's heads by Holly, fall off when the hunters and guides they were placed on slump over after being hit by an arrow.

Richard and Edward are the only ones who were not hit with an arrow.

The animals start to growl and roar as they inch closer to the dead hunting party.

There is an evil grin on Holly's face. "See, I told you not to worry." Holly pauses for a slight moment then,

"But then again, by the time I'm done with you, you're going to wish you had an arrow in your forehead."

The snow devil that brought Holly and her family to the hunters and their guides, reappears in a swirling motion.

Holly walks around to the front of Richard and Edward.

Prancer and Vixen lovingly take each other's hand and walk into the snow devil.

Eggnog picks up an apple and throws it at the head of one of the dead hunters before he too retreats into the snow devil.

Holly turns on her heels and without saying another word, she is the last to walk into the snow devil.

Richard, Edward, and their dead companions are left behind with the animals that are still gathered around them.

The animals do not move or make a sound. It's as if they are waiting for someone to give them permission to attack.

With fear still frozen on their faces, Richard and Edward exchange looks. Each one wondering if they are going to be attacked and eaten alive by the animals or will they have an arrow imbedded into their forehead as well.

As Richard and Edward both turn away from each other, a strong stench of a dead skunk and rotten fish market hits both the men in the face like a brick wall.

The stench is so bad, both men instantly throw up all over.

Richard falls to his hands and knees while still throwing up uncontrollably.

The ground in front of Richard is covered in his vomit.

Edward on the other hand, wipes his mouth and, "What the fuck." He looks around and notices all the animals are still watching him and Richard. He then looks

to the snow devil that is still spiraling around.
As Edward keeps watching the spiraling snow devil, a large footsteps through the snow devil then the rest of the body that belongs to the large foot.
Frostbite is so tall that he has to duck down to step all the way through the snow devil. Some of his head skims the top of the snow devil.
Edward is terrified and falls backwards in his chair, screaming.
Richard scurries, backwards as fast as he can, trying to get away from the beast coming through the snow devil.
Because of the animals still surrounding them, Richard and Edward don't get too far.

Moments later, Frostbite is walking back into the snow devil, dragging an unconscious Richard and Edward behind him.
The big cats are feeding on some of the dead hunters and guides while all the other animals are crushing the rest of the hunting party under their feet.

14

LAST OF THE PUPS

Late at night.
The Kringle kitchen was at one time used to make dozens upon dozens of pastries and all kinds of other baked goods for the citizens of Christmas Village.
The aroma of what was being cooked in the kitchen was so strong that you could smell it throughout all of Christmas Village; pies of every kind, Danishes, macarons, eclairs, strudels, cannolis, pretzels, croissants, donuts, cookies, and breads of every type.
It's been years since the Kringle kitchen has been used for any kind of cooking, which is until now.
Pepper has placed lit candles throughout the kitchen. It is what she likes to do when she cooks.
To some, this might be strange and unheard of but to Pepper, it's something that helps clear her mind and gives her a sense of peacefulness as she cooks.
Pepper is dressed in a body-hugging candy cane stripped thermal onesie that is showing off all her womanly curves. She also has an apron on that is decorated in a candy cane pattern.
Pepper's hair is disheveled as if it were put through a wind tunnel as she rummages through the pantry. She is loading her arms up with ingredients; dark brown sugar,

molasses, flower, baking soda, salt, ginger, cinnamon, nutmeg and all spice.

Once she has all the ingredients she is looking for, Pepper puts them on the countertop and then heads to the refrigerator for some butter and eggs.

It's not long before Pepper is beating the molasses, eggs and water into her creamed butter and brown sugar.

"Oh, I almost forgot the secret ingredient." Pepper pulls a vial of Mr. Heat's blood from an apron pocket and holds it up to a candle to inspect it. She turns the vial of blood a few times then smiles as she pours it into the bowl of ingredients she was just beating.

Pepper then beats the blood into the rest of the ingredients until there is a maroon colored dough in the bowl.

Forty minutes later, Pepper is covered in flower, dark brown sugar and sticky molasses as she pulls two cookie sheets out of the oven with three maroon colored gingerbread men on one cookie sheet and two on the other.

After the gingerbread men have cooled down enough, Pepper begins to decorate them with colored frosting, candies, and sprinkles to give them their own personalities.

A potbellied gingerbread man that Pepper is decorating starts to giggle as the frosting is tickling it.

Eggnog walks in on Pepper as she's decorating the gingerbread men. "Mmm... I thought I smelt something cooking." Eggnog reaches for one of the already decorated gingerbread men without asking.

The potbellied gingerbread man that was giggling, comes to life. "Fuck you, you little asshole. You take a bite out of me, and I'll bite your fucking tongue off and shit it in your mouth." The gingerbread man says in a high pitched voice.

The rest of the gingerbread men and a couple

gingerbread women jump to their feet. Some of them are decorated while others are waiting for their royal icing to be put on.

Eggnog quickly pulls his hand away. "Oh, shit! They're alive!" Eggnog says, surprisingly.

Pepper slaps Eggnog's hand without saying a word.

"HEY! What the hell was that for?" Eggnog grabs his hand.

"Yes they're alive, and unless you want to choke to death, I wouldn't eat them if I were you. Especially that one." Pepper points to the potbellied gingerbread man that's trying to stand up. "That one is mine. His name is Motherfucker or MOFO for short."

MOFO is decorated with royal icing. He has two white, round royal icing eyes and a white royal icing mouth. He also has a red and white bowtie made from royal icing and three round red circles going down the front of him and white squiggly lines on his wrists and ankle areas.

Later the next night.

An eighteen year old Sophia plugs in a curling iron then sets it on the bathroom vanity while it gets hot. She then walks out of the bathroom. "Come on guys. It's time for bed. Your mom and dad will be home soon. I want you in bed before they get home." Sophia hollers to the three kids she is babysitting.

The laughter of children can be heard coming from another room in the house.

Sophia walks back into the bathroom, frustrated that the kids won't listen to her. "Come on guys, let's get into bed so I can get ready for my date. Your mom and dad will be home soon."

As Sophia leans in close to the mirror to inspect her face, the three kids she is babysitting chase each other past the bathroom, screaming and laughing at each other.

Sophia quickly walks back out into the hallway and hollers to the kids once more. "COME ON GUYS! WHAT DID I SAY!"

Unknown to Sophia as she steps out of the bathroom, ice crystals are forming around the outer perimeter of one of the shower's glass doors.

The ice crystals make a cracking and creaking sound as they continue to work their way to the center of the glass door, until the door is completely covered in ice crystals.

The temperature in the bathroom also drops.

Again, Sophia walks back into the bathroom. This time, feeling defeated by the defying children, she hangs her head down. Sophia sighs then stands in front of the mirror.

Sophia notices the bathroom has gotten colder so she rubs her arms to warm them up. "Damn it's cold in here. Where'd all the heat go?" Sophia askes herself.

Sophia is still unaware of what's happening with the shower door.

Sophia rubs her arms some more as she looks at herself in the mirror. She looks at her teeth, making sure there isn't any food stuck in between them.

As Sophia leans closer into the mirror, she hears something creaking and cracking behind her. Without turning her head, Sophia looks behind her, in the mirror. She is surprised to see one of the shower doors is covered in ice crystals.

"What the hell!" Sophia quickly turns around. She sees a rough silhouette of someone behind the ice crystals.

The silhouette is getting closer as if it were walking towards the shower door.

Surprised and at a loss for words, Sophia slowly backs out of the bathroom without taking her eyes off the shower door.

Finally, as the silhouette gets closer, a woman's face starts to take shape within the ice crystals that have covered the shower door. The woman's face is white and powder blue in color. Her eyelashes and eyebrows are covered in small ice crystals. The woman's lips are somewhat of a blueish black color.

Then, a young Holly steps through the ice crystal covered shower door as if it were an open doorway. First Holly's head and arms then the rest of her body.

Holly is dressed in her powder blue Santa outfit.

Holly exhales, letting out a puff of cold air.

Sophia turns to run out of the bathroom screaming.

As Sophia gets no more than a few steps out of the bathroom, Holly grabs a handful of Sophia's hair and violently yanks her back. "How rude of you to run out on your guests. And I haven't even introduced myself yet."

Sophia kicks and screams. "PLEASE LET ME GO!" She screams again. "LET ME GO!"

Holly smashes Sophia's face into the mirror, shattering the mirror into hundreds of smaller pieces.

Sophia's face is cut up from the pieces of broken mirror.

"I'm here trying to be nice and friendly, but you won't let me do that." Holly viciously drags Sophia's face along the smashed mirror, first to the right then to the left.

The children are making so much noise that they don't even hear what's going on in the bathroom.

Sophia's face is bleeding profusely from being dragged along the smashed mirror. Her face is cut up from the broken pieces of mirror. She even has pieces of the mirror stuck in her face. Sophia nose is also shattered.

Sophia moans in pain as she cries.

"Next time you'll shut up and listen, won't you?" Holly asks Sophia before tossing her out of the bathroom and into the bedroom across from the bathroom as if Sophia

were some kind of rag doll.
Again, Sophia moans in pain and gasps for air as she crawls to the side of the bed, leaving a trail of blood behind her.
As Holly walks out of the bathroom, Eggnog is the next one to walk through the ice crystal covered shower door, wearing a brown monk's robe.
Eggnog walks out of the bathroom with a slight wabble to his walk.
When Eggnog reaches Holly, he stands to the side of her.
Holly and Eggnog hear the playful laughter of children in another part of the house. They both turn their heads to where the laughter is coming from.
Holly looks at Eggnog. "Go collect the pups. You can have their teeth but bring me what's left."
Eggnog smiles and turns on his heels as he hurries out of the bedroom. He pulls a small hammer from his belt as he leaves.
Holly looks down at Sophia who is lying in a pool of her own blood. Holly thinks for a moment then, "You know… It's nothing personal. We came for the pups. You're just in the wrong place, wrong time."
Sophia moans again then begs. "Please no. Please." Sophia cries.
Holly reaches down and picks Sophia up by the hair on her head and slams her onto the bed so that just her feet are hanging off the bed. Holly then reaches for the back of Sophia's pants and rips them off her in one motion.
Sophia bounces on the bed a few times from her pants being ripped off. She has no underwear on so she is now naked from the waist down.
Holly throws Sophia's ripped pants on the floor then walks back into the bathroom. She picks up the hot curling iron by its handle and yanks its cord out of the

outlet.

Holly returns to the bedroom with the curling iron in hand. When she reaches Sophia, Holly kicks Sophia's legs so they are wider apart.

On a nightstand by the bed, a family picture of a woman kissing the cheek of Santa Claus and three little children catches Holly's attention for a second.

Holly then turns to Sophia and grabs onto one of her shoulders for leverage and whispers in Sophia's ear. "Now hold still. This might hurt a bit." Holly tightens her grip on Sophia's shoulder and whispers in her ear again. "Oh, my mistake. This is going to hurt a lot."

With one hand on Sophia's shoulder, Holly thrusts all five inches of the curling iron's hot heating bar into Sophia's asshole.

There's a sizzling sound coming from Sophia's asshole as Holly moves around the heating bar in Sophia's asshole. You know, the same sizzling sound bacon makes as it's being cooked on a hot pan.

Smoke rises out of Sophia's asshole where the hot curling iron is stuffed into.

Sophia screams as if her soul is being ripped from her as Holly takes great joy in playing with the hot curling iron stuffed in Sophia's asshole.

Sophia flails around on the bed like a fish out of water, trying to get away but it does her no good. Holly is far stronger and therefor able to hold Sophia down until the life is burned from her.

Meanwhile, on the other side of town.

A light snowfall is coming down, adding to the snow that's already covering the ground while a slight winter breeze blows through the night.

As Nancy tries to corral her four children for showers and bed, she hears a light knock on the front door,

Nancy listens for the knock again just to make sure she wasn't hearing things.

And again, there is a light knock on the front door.

Nancy isn't expecting anyone at this hour and her husband isn't due home from his hunting trip with Richard for another few days so she wonders who it could be.

When Nancy reaches the front door, she turns on the outside light then looks out one of the windows to see who's knocking on her door before opening it.

Nancy sees a young woman with a pale complexion, rosy, red cheeks, and bright red lipstick. The woman's red and white hair reminds Nancy of a candy cane.

The woman is wearing what looks to be a mini dress that's being covered up by a buttoned up, over-sized hooded parka over coat with a stitched burgundy and white patchwork pattern. The coat also has white fur trim around the hood, zipper area, and wrists.

Nancy's eyes are also drawn to the woman's knee-high white fur leg warmers that also have red and white striped ties with white pom-poms. Red and white candy canes also decorate the front and back of the leg warmers.

The woman has some type of crown on her head made from vines and adorned with; pinecones, pine needles, cranberries, and candy canes.

The woman is holding a red and white candy cane striped gift bag.

A winter breeze is blowing the woman's candy cane colored hair all around. Tufts of the woman's hair is blowing into her crown. She brushes away some hair from her face.

Nancy thinks to herself, "What a strange looking woman."

The woman notices Nancy peering out at her through a window. The woman smiles and gives a friendly wave.

Nancy quickly steps away from the window and thinks for a moment. "What harm can a woman dressed like a candy cane be?" Nancy asks herself. She then decides to open the door.

As soon as Nancy opens the door, she is hit in the face with a strong peppermint candy cane aroma. The aroma is so strong, Nancy can taste it on her lips.

Before Nancy can say one word to the woman standing in front of her, the woman offers Nancy her hand to shake and introduces herself.

"Hi, my name is Peppermint, but my friends call me Pepper." Pepper gives Nancy's hand a few quick shakes before letting go of her hand.

"Hello." Nancy responds with a puzzled look on her face. She doesn't know if she should go back in the house and slam the door in Pepper's face or stay and see what she wants.

Before Nancy makes up her mind on what to do, Pepper finishes her introduction. "I just moved in down the street a few days ago. I don't know anyone around here so, I thought I'd walk around the neighborhood and introduce myself. I brought some candy canes and homemade gingerbread men." As Pepper hands the red and white candy cane striped gift bag to Nancy, the hairs on Pepper's body stands on end. Even the hair on her head starts to stick up.

Nancy takes the gift bag with a smile. "Thank you."

Meanwhile, Nancy's four children run up behind their mother, trying to see who is at the door.

Each child is holding a toy; a stuffed white elephant with pink polka dots, a little doll with red hair, a little blue train, and a blue plane.

"Oooh, she's pretty. Who is she mommy?" One of Nancy's little girls blurts out.

No one notices the little doll with red hair come to life in the little girl's hand as it waves to Pepper. No one but Pepper that is.

Pepper smiles at the little girl even though the smile is meant for the little doll.

One of Nancy's little boys sniffles a couple times as if he were smelling something. "She smells like a candy cane."

Pepper's smile grows as a result of the children's remarks.

"Kids, now don't be rude." Nancy gently moves one of her little girls behind her.

Pepper kneels so that she is eye level to Nancy's children. "Oh, these are such cute pups. Are they yours?" Pepper asks Nancy as she waves at the children.

All four of the children wave back while smiling.

"Excuse me?" Nancy asks Pepper with a puzzled expression on her face as she looks at her children then back to Pepper.

Pepper looks up at Nancy. Then, as she stands up. "Oh, I'm sorry. Where I come from, up north, they call little children, pups." Pepper smiles at Nancy.

Nancy looks in the gift bag filled with gingerbread men and candy canes. She then turns to her children who are still amused by Pepper. Nancy looks back at Pepper and asks, "Do you want to come in and maybe have some hot chocolate and share some of the treats you brought?"

Pepper's eyes widen with excitement. "Sure, I'd love to."

All four of Nancy's children holler with excitement. "YAY!"

Nancy's two little girls quickly grab each of Pepper's hands and escorts her into the house while the two boys run ahead of them.

Pepper whispers under her breath as she walks into

the house, looking at the children. "Now for the rest of the pups."

Nancy shuts the door.

As Pepper walks into the house, she takes in all the Christmas decorations that are still up.

"Okay, guys, be nice and show our guest to the living room while I make some hot chocolate." Nancy tells her children as she walks to the kitchen.

Nancy's children drop their toys as they walk further into the house.

Nancy's two girls walk Pepper into the living room, occasionally looking up and exchanging smiles with Pepper while Nancy's two sons have already found a spot on the couch to sit.

Nancy hollers from the kitchen. "Please excuses all the Christmas decoration. We're a little late taking them down."

"Oh, that's okay. I actually love the Christmas season and everything about it. It's the most wonderful time of the year." Pepper hollers back as an all-white and silver Christmas tree in the far corner of the living room catches her eye.

There's a bright twinkle in Pepper's eyes as she is enthralled with the all-white and silver Christmas tree. It has been a long time since she has seen a beautifully decorated Christmas tree as beautiful as the one in front of her.

There are all kinds of silvery glitter bulbs of all shapes and sizes hung from the Christmas tree, white bulbs with silver glitter as well. There are white bows and silver bows all over the white tree. Silver snowflakes and white snowflakes hang from the tree branches. White doves have been neatly placed within the branches of the Christmas tree.

When it comes to illuminating the Christmas tree,

Nancy and her family didn't use the normal, everyday string of lights. The Christmas tree is lit up with lots of LED fairy lights.

The cherry on top of the tree is a silver beaded and glittered star-shaped metal treetop that's lit up with the same kind of fairy lights that are strung around the tree.

Pepper looks down and notices a partially unwrapped jack-in-the-box that no one seemed to want, still under the tree.

The jack-in-the-box is decorated with a snowy winter wonderland scenery with silver and gold trim.

So that no one hears her, Pepper whispers to the jack-in-the-box. "Hello Charlie."

One of Nancy's little girls takes Pepper's hand and walks her back to the couch where Pepper sits in between the two boys who are waiting with big smiles.

Nancy walks in with two cups of hot chocolate and the bag of candy canes and gingerbread men.

Nancy sets the hot chocolates and bag of treats on a table in front of the couch. "I didn't know if you wanted marshmallows so, I just put some in one cup. You can take which ever one you want."

"Oh, thank you. I do love marshmallows in my hot chocolate." Pepper says as she grabs the hot chocolate with the marshmallows in it.

Nancy's four children are gathered in close around Pepper.

Pepper takes a sip of her hot chocolate. She quickly turns her head away from Nancy and makes a face as if she had just taken a sip of a strong bitter tasting coffee.

The marshmallows are also hard and stale.

Because she is preoccupied with her kids, Nancy doesn't see Pepper making her face.

"Come on guys, back away from Pepper and give her some room. I'm sure she doesn't want a bunch of kids climbing all over her." Nancy says as she tries to gently pull one of her daughters away from Pepper.

Pepper quickly puts her cup of hot chocolate down. "Oh, that's okay. I love pu... I love children." Pepper quickly corrects herself.

Frustrated at her children's behavior, "Kevin and Gary, what are you doing smelling her hair? Stop it."

"But mom, she smells good." Kevin sticks his nose is Pepper's hair and sniffs long and hard.

"Yea, she smells like a candy cane." Gary says with a big smile and bright eyes.

Pepper finds all this attention amusing.

Nancy points to her children. "Settle down and I'll let you have the gingerbread men and candy canes that Pepper brought us."

There are a few seconds of silence as if the children were thinking what to do next. Then they quickly find a place to sit and wait for their treats.

Nancy first hands her children a candy cane.

It doesn't take long for the children to unwrap and eat their candy canes.

"Come on guys, it's not a race. Did you even taste the candy canes?" Nancy asks her children.

Nancy's children just giggle.

"Boy, they love candy canes, don't they?" Pepper asks Nancy as she watches the children.

"They'll eat anything that's sweet. They get that from their father." Nancy says as she takes a sip of her hot chocolate.

Pepper sits up. "Their father? Where's he at?" Pepper asks even though she knows full well where he's at.

"Oh, he's off on some big game hunting trip." Nancy takes another sip of her hot chocolate.

Pepper has lost the taste for her hot chocolate, so she doesn't bother drinking any more of hers.

"Can we have a gingerbread man cookie" One of Nancy's daughters asks as all the children sit with their hands held out, waiting for a delicious gingerbread cookie.
Nancy thinks for a moment then, "Alright, a gingerbread man cookie then off to bed." Nancy picks up the bag of gingerbread men cookies and looks in the bag. "Oooh! They smell delicious." Nancy says as she pulls the gingerbread men out one at a time and hands them to her children. She hands her little girls a gingerbread woman.
"Thank you. It's a family recipe." Pepper says with a big smile.
Just as the children are about to devour their cookies, Nancy stops them. "You guys know better than that. What are you guys supposed to say?" Nancy asks her children.
All the children look at Pepper with wide eyes and candy cane encrusted smiles. "Thank you." The children all say at the same time then turn to their mother and wait for permission to eat their cookies.
Pepper and Nancy smile at the children.
"Go ahead, you can eat them." Nancy tells her children.
The children devour their gingerbread men just as fast as they ate their candy canes. It's as if they had never eaten before.
When the children are done, the only trace of there being candy canes and gingerbread men are the children's candy cane and gingerbread men encrusted mouth and a few crumbs lying about on the floor.
With a mischievous smile, "There should be one in the bag for you too." Pepper point to the candy cane stripped bag.
"Oh no. I couldn't." Nancy kindly declines Pepper's offer as she takes another sip of her hot chocolate.
"Come on, I made enough for everyone." Pepper

insists as the hairs on her arms stand at attention.

Nancy puts her cup of hot chocolate down then, "Oh, okay. They do smell delicious."

Nancy watches her children rolling around on the living room floor. She lets them have their fun even though she said they had to go to bed after they had their gingerbread men.

As Nancy opens the bag that had the gingerbread men and candy canes in it, a high-pitched voice is heard coming from the bottom of the bag.

The voice in the bag threatens Nancy. "I don't think so bitch. You eat me, I'm going to shred your fucking asshole up when I come out your backend."

Startled, Nancy drops the bag and looks up, she now notices that her children are not playing. Instead, they are clutching their swollen throats as they gasp for air. A couple of the children have even turned a shade of blue.

Nancy doesn't see the round and thick gingerbread man crawling out of the bag she had just dropped.

As Nancy turns to Pepper with a shocked expression, Pepper thrusts a pointed candy cane from her crown, into Nancy's temple.

Nancy falls back into her chair with a candy cane buried deep in her temple while most of her children now lie motionless on the living room floor.

MOFO kicks Nancy's ankle. "Stupid bitch. That's what you get for dropping me."

Some time has passed since Pepper was invited into Nancy's house.

Pepper has turned off all the lights in the house except for the lights on the all-white and silver Christmas tree. She is now sitting back on the couch and enjoying the Christmas tree.

Pepper closes her eyes and listens. There's a slight

wheezing sound coming from two of the children.

Nancy's children have consumed all the candy canes and gingerbread men they were given to them by Pepper. All that's left are gingerbread men crumbs scattered about on the living room rug and maybe a little piece of a candy cane, here and there.

Everyone is now lying on the floor, clutching their throats that are stuffed and bloated with candy canes and gingerbread men. Their eyes are bulging out of their sockets. Two of the children are gagging and coughing while the other two are not moving at all.

Nancy isn't moving at all.

There's a blueish hue to the children's complexion.

A few of the gingerbread men that were eaten have come to life and are now trying to climb out of the mouths they are in.

Pepper sits back on the couch and admires her handy work while MOFO stands on her left shoulder, wickedly laughing.

"Fucking beautiful." MOFO continues his wicked laughing.

Charlie the jack-in-the-box is on the couch beside Pepper. His crank has been wound, setting him free from his metal prison.

Charlie is a clown that has got powder blue hair that's wild and windblown even though he hasn't been out in the wind or any kind of breeze let alone out of his box in a very long time.

Charlie has a white face with a big powder blue nose and a big powder blue smile to match his hair. He also has black diamonds painted over both of his eyes.

Charlie's clothes consists of just a baggy long sleeved shirt that's white with black and powder blue circles. He also has a bow tie with small powder blue circles all over it.

Small white cotton gloves completes Charlie's outfit.

Charlie smiles from ear to ear as a deep cynical laugh seems to be coming out of his mouth.

15

DADDY DEAREST

Dean Street in the Spitalfields District of London England, 1844. Just before Sunset, in the middle of winter.

A brisk winter breeze is making a whistling sound as it rattles the paper thin windows of a small old hattery that's been closed for some time now.

Genevieve walks up to one of the windows of the hattery. Her long black hair blowing in the wind.

The cold weather doesn't seem to be bothering Genevieve as she is wearing just an elegant, crimson and black Victorian dress with nothing on her feet.

So that she can see in, Genevieve brushes off some of the snow and ice that has accumulated on the window.

With no source of light in the hattery, Genevieve is finding it hard to see much of anything inside the small hattery.

As she strains to look inside, Genevieve sees an old wooden table that's littered with all kinds of tools that a hatter would use. There are even a few tattered and torn hats on the table as well.

As Genevieve continues to look inside the hattery, she sees a couple wooden standing hat racks with all kinds of top hats hanging from them.

From the looks of it, the little old hattery hasn't

seen any kind of business for quite some time. There are chairs tipped over along with material used to make hats, scattered all over the floor.

Because some of the windows of the hattery are broken, snow has found its way in. There's snow piled up on the floor, on the shelves and on the tables. You can even see some snow blowing around inside the hattery as if it were falling from the hattery's ceiling.

Then, in the far corner of the hattery, sitting in front of a small coal hearth that looks like it hasn't been used in a while, is a little old man with a thin and tattered blanket wrapped around him. There is snow all over the old man. His skin is blueish gray.

Genevieve knows it's too late but still, she softly taps on the paper thin window to try and get the old man's attention.

The old man ignores Genevieve's tapping. He just sits in front of his coal hearth.

Genevieve starts to cry. "Oh, Abraham. I'm so sorry." Genevieve whispers to her boyfriend. As she turns to face a six foot tall snowman wearing a silk top hat with tears in her eyes, "We're too late."

The snowman absorbs Genevieve's body into his as he quickly rushes to the same window that Genevieve was looking through.

As the snowman looks through the window, "We'll make him pay for what he has done." Genevieve says from inside the snowman.

The snowman screams and loses its density as it smashes through the window and rushes into the hattery, causing a blizzard inside.

Seconds later, the blizzard stops and the snowman takes shape beside his dead father.

Meanwhile, on the other side of town where the rich

upper class live.

Augustus has lost many people over the years that were close to him, both family and friends.

It's been thirty-three years since the death of Augustus' daughter, Genevieve and even longer for the passing of his wife who was murdered in her sleep.

Hell, Most of Augustus' rich friends have either died or are too old to even remember who Augustus is.

Now, a sixty-nine-year-old Augustus is in his hunting cabin, siting in an old, worn parlor chair built out of mahogany wood and upholstered in crimson red velvet with a rose pattern. Some of the finish on the mahogany arm rests of the chair has worn away from the years of use. There's also worn marks on the upholstery part of the arm rests as well. The seat of the chair has lost its nice, soft cushiony feel that it once had so long ago. Now, the seat of the chair is flat and concaved, causing Augustus to sit lower in his chair.

Even though his chair is a bit uncomfortable, Augustus is enjoying the warmth of a roaring fireplace while sipping on his Old Tom Gin.

As he takes a few sips, Augustus looks at the heads of his big game trophies that are mounted on the walls of his hunting cabin; an elephant, a grizzly bear, a lion, a blue wildebeest, a big horn sheep, an American bison, and a cape buffalo.

Augustus takes another sip of his Old Tom Gin and then sighs. "Oh, what great times I had." Augustus says to himself, referring to hunting down all the animals that are now hanging on his cabin walls.

Augustus takes the last sip of his Old Tom Gin then sets his empty glass down by the half bottle of Old Tom Gin that's on a stand by his chair.

Augustus rests his arms on the worn arm rests of his parlor chair, sits back and closes his eyes.

It's not too long after Augustus closes his eyes that he falls into an alcohol induced sleep.

The memories of his various hunting expeditions fade away and are soon replaced by those of his deceased wife who was murdered in her sleep.

There's a shadow of someone standing over Augustus' wife while she sleeps. The shadow picks up a pillow and forcefully places it over Augustus' wife's face.

Augustus' wife wakes up out of her sleep, thrashing her arms and legs. She fights to get the pillow off her face, but she cannot. Her attacker is stronger than she is as he holds her head down with the pillow, covering her face.

Augustus' wife tries to scream for her husband, but her screams are muffled by the pillow over her face.

Then after a minute or two... silence.

Augustus' wife is no longer thrashing around or screaming. She is silent and still as if she had gone back to sleep.

In another alcohol induced dream, Augustus is standing in a dark room, void of all light except for a soft white glow shining down on him from an unknown source, somewhere above him.

Augustus is holding his Blunderbuss out in front of him. He fires into the darkness.

There's a loud explosion as gray and white smoke bellows out from the Blunderbuss and surrounds Augustus.

The sound of the Blunderbuss firing startles Augustus in his sleep, causing him to knock over his empty glass and the half bottle of Old Tom Gin.

The glass and half bottle of Old Tom Gin shatter upon hitting the floor.

The sound of the glass and bottle breaking wakes

Augustus up. He sits up in his chair and looks at the mess on the floor. "Damn it." Augustus says in a whisper.

A few minutes later, Augustus hears three light knocks on his cabin door. He quickly looks at the cabin door and sighs out of frustration, then, "I left word at the house that I didn't want to be disturbed."

No one answers Augustus.

Again, there are three light knocks on the cabin door.

Augustus grips both arm rests of his chair and uses them for support as he jumps to his feet. "DAMN IT! I SAID…" Augustus rushes to the cabin door.

This time, there is an answer. An answer that cuts Augustus off as he reaches for the cabin's door handle.

"Not even for your little girl, daddy?" A woman speaks to Augustus from the other side of the cabin door.

With his hand inches from the door handle, the woman's words make Augustus stop dead in his tracks.

Augustus is in shock as his mouth drops open. He recognizes the woman's voice, but it can't be because daddy's little girl died years ago.

Genevieve died years ago.

"Daddy, it's so cold out here. Please let me in so I can get warm. I'm freezing." The woman begs Augustus.

Augustus turns back to grab his Blunderbuss on a wall mount. "I don't know who the fuck you are but you're not my daughter." Augustus quickly loads his Blunderbuss. "My daughter died a while ago."

"No daddy, I didn't die. You killed me. You killed me and Abraham just like you killed mommy. You remember mommy, don't you daddy?" There are a few seconds of silence then the woman continues. "You put a pillow over her face while she slept and kept it there until she stopped kicking and screaming."

Augustus whips open the cabin door and fires his

Blunderbuss before finding out who is on the other side of the door.

The shot from the Blunderbuss blows the head and upper torso off a six-foot snowman.

The snowman's silk top hat flies through the air and lands in a nearby snowbank, out of Augustus' line of site.

Augustus is surprised to find just a partial snowman outside of his hunting cabin. He wonders where the woman went to so fast in all the deep snow.

Augustus steps out of his warm cabin and looks around for the woman. He sees no tracks of any kind.

With his Blunderbuss in hand, Augustus walks back into his cabin with a puzzled look on his face. He slams the door, wondering if the woman's voice was the result of all the Old Tom Gin that he had drank. Augustus then asks himself, "If the woman's voice was the result of all the Old Tom Gin, then who made the six-foot snowman that he just blew away?"

Augustus puts a hand on his head as he leans back on the closed door. "I really have to stop drinking." He tells himself.

"When you killed Abraham, you also caused his father to die of a broken heart. You shouldn't have killed us daddy." There's a slight pause then, "Now it's your turn."

Augustus quickly takes his hand away from his head. He is surprised to hear the woman's voice again.

Augustus drops his Blunderbuss.

A strong wind starts to blow and violently shakes the door and walls of Augustus' hinting cabin. The windows vibrate so much from the wind that they're making a humming sound.

Augustus turns to look at the cabin door as he jumps away from it.

Augustus has got a horrific expression on his face. His hands are trembling.

Augustus trips over his blunderbuss as he takes a couple steps back and falls back onto his ass.

The wind stops blowing the door and walls of the cabin.

Then there is silence.

It is now so silent in Augustus' hunting cabin that he can hear his heart rapidly beating. If Augustus' heart were beating any faster, it would explode right out of his chest.

Augustus takes a moment to catch his breath and just when he thinks it's over, the cabin door explodes into thousands of splinters. The windows shatter, sending shards of glass everywhere.

Augustus covers his face.

A light, fluffy snowfall is coming in through the blown-out windows and what used to be the front door.

Augustus cautiously removes his hands from his eyes and face and looks around at the mess that the shattered windows and door have made.

There's shattered glass and pieces of the cabin door everywhere. Some of Augustus' wall mounted big game trophies have got large pieces of the door sticking out of them.

Augustus' face and hands are cut up and bleeding from the flying glass and splintered door.

Augustus looks out to where the front door used to be. He sees a light snowfall coming down.

A gust of wind blows around the old silk top hat that was on the snowman's head. The top hat blows around in the air a few times before gently setting down in the snow, a few feet in front of what used to be the cabin door.

Augustus rubs his eyes in disbelief as he sits up. "What the fuck!"

Another gust of wind picks the silk top hat up and blows it around in a spiral pattern, six feet into the air, taking snow with it.

Snow that was taken up with the top hat starts to take the shape of a snowman. First the snowman's lower half, mind section then finally, the snowman's head.

The old silk top hat comes to rest on the snowman's head. Two gnarly sticks for arms slowly protrude out on either side of the snowman's upper body.

The snowman doesn't have two pieces of coal for eyes or a carrot for a nose that a normal snowman of today would have. But then again, having just two circular indentations in his head where his eyes would be, if he had eyes and three huge sections to his body that brings his height to six feet tall, the snowman that stands before Augustus is anything but normal.

The snowman's eyebrows are pushed down in the middle and raised on the side, giving him an angry looking expression.

The snowman's mouth starts to move and what come out of the snowman's mouth shocks Augustus even more especially since snowmen aren't supposed to talk. "HAPPY BITHDAY, MOTHERFUCKER!" The snowman says in a deep voice.

Augustus is at a loss for words as he has never heard a snowman talk before.

"Oh, daddy dearest and still you don't invite us in. What's the matter daddy? Don't you love your little girl anymore?" The woman's voice is now coming from the snowman.

Even though he is stricken with fear, Augustus' face turns hard and rigid. "SHUT THE FUCK UP! MY LITTLE GIRL NEVER CALLED ME DADDY!"

"You're right." The woman's voice says.

The snowman loses his density and turns into a powdery snow that falls to the ground, starting with his head and slowly works its way down until all that's left is a woman standing in the snowman's place, a woman Augustus knows all too well. A woman who goes by the name, Genevieve, Augustus' daughter.

The snowman's old silk hat gently drops on Genevieve's head.

Augustus cannot believe his eyes. His long dead daughter stands before him but yet her body was buried in the family cemetery thirty-three years ago.

Genevieve stands before her father, barefoot and wearing the same elegant, crimson and black Victorian dress she was killed in.

Genevieve has a light brown, leather quiver with ten arrows in it, suspended from a belt around her waist. She is also holding an elaborately decorated, wooden longbow.

Augustus sits up. His mouth and eyes widen. He takes a deep breath as he thinks to himself. "This cannot be."

Without looking, Genevieve plucks an arrow from her quiver with her left hand and puts it to her longbow. She points the arrow at her father while drawing the arrow and bowstring.

"I called you, dad." Genevieve releases the arrow and bowstring.

Before Augustus can exhale the deep breath that he took, Genevieve's arrow finds its mark on the bridge of Augustus' nose, killing Augustus where his sits.

Present time.

There is a light snowfall coming down as Brian and his wife are traveling down an unlit back road in Brian's pick-up truck.

There is an uncomfortable silence in Brian's truck.

Jamie is staring out at the night sky. She is watching the snow slowly fall from the night sky as she thinks about the death of her father, mother, and sister and how much she misses then.

As Brian drives down the road, he can't see his wife's face with her looking the other way but he can tell she is crying.

Jamie sniffles and then wipes her eyes with the sleeve of her arm.

Brian doesn't know what he could say that could possibly ease the pain that his wife is feeling right now so, he takes his eyes off the road long enough to look at Jamie and gently lay a hand on her shoulder.

Jamie turns to look at Brian. There are no words, just a look of sadness.

Jamie's eyes are red, swollen and filled with tears. Her make-up is smeared all over her face. Jamie's cheeks and nose are red and blotchy. Her lips are quivering as she tries not to make a sound.

Then, out of the corner of her eye, Jamie notices, a little ways down the road, in front of them, a six-foot-tall snowman is standing in the middle of the road.

The snowman has got a silk top hat on, two pieces of coal for eyes, a gnarly orange carrot for a nose, a red and green scarf blowing in the winter breeze, and two long gnarled twigs for arms.

Jamie quickly braces her hands on the dashboard and screams. "BRIAN!"

Brian quickly looks in front of him. "WHAT THE FUCK!" Upon seeing the snowman in the middle of the road, Brian slams on the brakes to keep from hitting the snowman.

Brian's truck hits a patch of black ice and fish tails his truck a few times before coming to a stop about two car lengths in front of the snowman, head on.

While white knuckling the steering wheel, Brian quickly looks at Jamie who still has her hands on the dashboard with her head down.

Jamie is breathing heavy.

Concerned, Brian asks, "Are you okay?"

Without saying a word, Jamie nods her head, yes.

Brian turns his attention back to the snowman in the middle of the road. "Who the fuck put that thing in the road?"

Jamie has still got her head down with her eyes closed. She can feel her heart beating through her chest.

Brian looks out the driver's window and then the passenger window in hopes that he might spot the person who put the snowman in the road.

As Brian turns back to look at the snowman, a woman's bare leg slowly steps out of the snowman's torso, followed by the rest of the woman's body until she is standing between the snowman and Brian's truck.

The woman's hair is pitch black and in long dreadlocks that go to the middle of her back.

She is wearing a low-cut white, sleeveless trumpet gothic Victorian dress that is adorned with vintage lace mesh. Under the woman's dress, she is wearing a white bloomer with layered ruffle lace trim and a bow ribbon on the outer thigh portion of her bloomer.

A traditional, soft white leather, all in one bracer and bow glove with ruby red laces covers the woman's right forearm and three of her fingers.

The woman is holding an elaborately decorated, sixty-four inch long, wooden long bow made out of white oak, in her right hand. She also has a quiver full of arrows made of solid ice slung over her right shoulder.

Back in London, England her name was Genevieve. Now… she goes by the name of Cupid.

Brian cannot believe what just happened. "WHAT THE FUCK!" Brian leans a little more forward to get a better look at the woman who just stepped out of the six-foot snowman in the middle of the road.

Before Brian has the chance to do or say anything, Cupid plucks an ice arrow out of her quiver and draws it back on her bow and then releases it, all in one fluent motion and all done in the blink of an eye.

The arrow cuts through the winter air and within seconds of being released, it pierces the windshield of Brian's truck as if the windshield wasn't even there.

The ice arrow hits Brian between his eyes.

And just as quick as the first arrow, a second arrow is shot through the passenger side of the windshield and buries itself in the middle of Jamie's forehead before she even realizes what happened to her and Brian.

16

SEVERED BLOODLINE

    Elsewhere, at a small mom and pop grocery store, Bruce and his mother are going to do a little shopping.
    As they walk up to the front door of the store, Bruce, and his mother notice two identical women sucking on candy canes and wearing all white trench coats and white leather high platform boots while riding a coin operated horse just off to the side of the store's entrance.
    The two women are on the same horse, one behind the other. The woman in the back has got her arms wrapped around the woman in front of her.
    The two women move in a seductive, rhythmic movement as the coin operated horse slowly moves up and down.
    The two women smile and wave at Bruce.
    With a disgusted look on her face, Bruce's mother pulls Bruce in closer to her as they quickly walk into the store.
    A small antique brass bell hung over the store's front door rings as Bruce and his mother walk in.
    Once in the store, Bruce turns around as his mother walks on to do her shopping.
    Through the store's picture window, Bruce can see the coin operated horse but not the two women.

The two women have disappeared.

Bruce's mother hollers for him to catch up. "Come on Bruce, we have shopping to do."

Bruce catches up to his mother but then stops by the penny candy aisle with a big smile. He can smell the sweetness of all the candy in the air as he breathes in deeply through his nose.

Bruce hurries and tugs on his mother's coat before she disappears down another aisle. "Mom, can I get some candy? Please?"

Bruce's mom stops, turns around and greets Bruce with a warm smile. "What did you say, Bruce?" She asks.

"Can I have some candy, mom?" Bruce points to the aisle of penny candy.

Bruce's mom looks at the many bins of candy then she looks at a wide-eyed Bruce.

Bruce backs up into the candy aisle.

Even though Bruce's mother smiles at Bruce, she is hiding a heavy heart, a heavy heart that is filled with the painful loss of her father, mother, and sister.

Normally, Bruce's mother would have told him no to the candy but after everything they've been through as of late, she hasn't the heart to tell Bruce no. "A little candy won't hurt."

Bruce runs over to his mother and gives her a big hug. "Thanks, mom."

Bruce's mother can feel her eyes well up as she gently pats Bruce on the back. "Now you can get some candy but not a lot. Understand?"

Bruce let's go of his mother and as he hurries over to the candy, "Yes, mom." Bruce picks up a small paper bag used to put the penny candy in.

"When you're finished getting your candy, I'll be in the next aisle looking for a hickory honey ham in a can. Okay?" Bruce's mother tells Bruce before walking off to do her shopping.

The words that were just spoken to Bruce by his mother are nothing more than just a distant breeze in Bruce's ears as his eyes widen with excitement as he sees all the candy in front of him; Tootsie Rolls, Candy Sticks, Atomic Fireballs, Bit-O-Honey, Candy Buttons, Candy Necklaces, Peppermints, Pixy Stix, Bottle Caps and many more.

Bruce opens his small paper bag as he walks up to the bins of candy. He licks his lips as he thinks about what candy he wants to put in his bag first.

The small antique brass bell hung over the store's front door rings as a customer walks in.

After staring at the candy for what seems like hours, Bruce finally makes up his mind on what sweet treat he wants to put in his paper bag first. He reaches for the Bottle Caps.

An odor unlike all the other sweet-smelling candy in the aisle makes Bruce pause for a second before reaching into the Bottle Cap bin.

Bruce breathes in deeply. The smell of warm apple cider and cinnamon fills Bruce's nose.

This is usually something Bruce smells around Christmas time in his grandmother's house as she prepares Christmas dinner.

While enjoying the smell of warm apple cider and cinnamon, Bruce reaches into the Bottle Cap bin and pulls out a few Bottle Cap candies.

An old, heavy-set woman dressed in a powder blue, Santa Claus styled dress, trimmed in white fur walks up quietly behind Bruce.

The woman's head and face are hidden by a powder blue hood that's attached to a capelet. White satin mittens cover the woman's hands.

In a soft gentle voice, "Bottle Caps is it?"

Not recognizing the woman's voice as his mother's, Bruce quickly turns around and takes a step back, away from the strange woman.

Bruce drops the Bottle Caps that he has in his hand. The Bottle Caps roll to the woman's feet. The woman looks down at her feet. She watches as five Bottle Caps roll to her feet. The woman then looks at the little boy who dropped the sweet treats.

"My favorite candy is the lemon drops. They used to be my husband's favorite too." The woman says as she takes a step towards Bruce.

Bruce in return, takes another step back, away from the woman.

"Oh, I'm sorry, Bruce." The woman apologizes as she takes one of her mittens off and then slowly pulls her hood off.

The woman has a matching, powder blue Santa hat with white fur trim on under the hood.

The woman's white and gray hair is neatly stuffed into the Santa hat. Her face is wrinkled, and timeworn.

If only the wrinkles could talk, they would tell stories of the woman's past, a past filled with so much happiness and joy. A time before there was so much anger and sadness coursing through her veins.

The woman's blue eyes have a twinkle in them as she looks through her gold rectangular glasses.

Bruce takes a deep breath before speaking. "You know my name?" His eyes widen with excitement.

The woman's clothing is a different color than what Bruce is used to, but he soon realizes who the woman is, standing in front of him. "You're… You're… You're…"

Bruce can't seem to finish what he wants to say, so the woman helps him out. She offers her unmittened hand to Bruce to shake. "How rude of me. My name is Holly Kringle, but you can call me Holly." Holly smiles and waits for Bruce to put his little hand in hers to shake. "Go ahead, I won't bite."

Bruce looks at Holly's hand then remembers what his mother told him many times about strangers. "My mom told me to never talk to strangers." Bruce puts his hands behind his back while still holding onto his paper bag that has yet to have candy put into it.

Holly smiles. "Well, we're not strangers now, are we? You now know my name and I know yours."

Bruce and Holly exchange smiles then, "Have you been an angel all year?" Holly asks Bruce.

Meanwhile, Bruce's mother is still in the next aisle. She is reading the label on a can of hickory honey ham when she hears Bruce talking to someone in the next aisle over.

Bruce's mother hurries to the candy aisle to see who Bruce is talking to.

Even though the candy aisle is just one aisle over, by the time Bruce's mother reaches the candy aisle, Bruce is the only one in the aisle.

Bruce is holding his empty paper bag while looking up and down the candy aisle as if he were looking for something or someone.

Bruce's mother puts her hands on her hips. "Who were you talking to?" She asks with a puzzled look on her face.

Bruce looks at his mother. "Mrs. Kringle. But she said I could call her Holly."

Bruce's mother looks at her son sternly. "How many times have I told you to never talk to strangers?" She taps her foot on the ground.

"But mom, she isn't a stranger. It was Mrs. Kringle. You know, Santa's wife. She even knew my name." Bruce explains to his mother as he is still looking up and down the candy aisle.

Bruce's mother points a finger at her son. "Stop it. I don't want you talking to anymore strangers. Understand?"

Bruce continues to argue why he was talking to a stranger. "But mom, Holly said she has a surprise for me and you."

Bruce's mother now looks up and down the candy aisle. "Well, where is she then? Where is this surprise this lady has for us?"

Bruce puts his hands in the air. "I don't know. She poof, disappeared when she heard you coming."

Any other day, Bruce's mother would have tanned her son's ass for telling a story like this but after burring three family members, she just hasn't got the heart to do it. So instead, she gives Bruce a stern warning. "If you tell anymore stories like that again, I'm going to tan your ass. Do you understand?"

Disappointed, Bruce lowers his head and shakes his head, yes.

After shopping, Bruce and his mother are driving down an old, dark country road with only the lights from the car and the full moon over head to sine the way where they are going.

Bruce is sitting in the back seat without his seatbelt on. He is taking great pleasure in smelling his bag of penny candy and then counting each piece.

Bruce's mother looks in her rear-view mirror and notices that Bruce hasn't got his seat belt on. She takes her eyes off the road long enough so that she can turn around to look at Bruce. "Put that seat belt on… NOW!"

Upon hearing his mother, Bruce quickly looks up from his bag of candy to see his mother looking at him until someone standing on the side of the road catches Bruce's attention as they drive by.

Bruce's mother turns back around after warning

Bruce. She doesn't see the person standing on the side of the road that Bruce had just seen.

Ignoring his mother, Bruce quickly sits up and looks back. "WAIT! STOP MOM!" With great excitement in his voice, "That's Holly, the lady I was talking to in the store." Bruce points at the woman standing on the side of the road.

Bruce's mother quickly looks in her side mirror and then in her rear-view mirror.

Holly watches Bruce and his mother speed by.

Bruce's mother looks in the rear-view mirror just in time to see the power blue blur of someone standing on the side of the road. Bruce's mother can't make out who it is because their head and face are hidden by a hood.

Bruce screams. "MOM!"

Two reindeer cows run across the road and disappear into the snow-covered woods.

Bruce's mother slams on the brakes.

Hitting some ice on the road, the car spins out of control which in return causes the car to violently roll several times

Bruce is thrown through the windshield, face first and is now lying in a snowbank along the side of the road.

There are small shards of glass protruding out from Bruce's face. His face and hands are badly cut up and bleeding. Bruce's nose is also broken and bleeding profusely. A good chunk of the windshield is sticking out of Bruce's right eye. Both of Bruce's legs are bent in opposite directions that they are not meant to be bent in.

The hickory smoked ham in a can that Bruce's mother bought has also been thrown from the car and is now rolling across the icy road until it stops and falls on its side.

The car comes to a stop, upside down, wrapped around a tree. Smoke is bellowing out from under the hood of the car. The windshield and all the other windows are smashed out.

Because of her seat belt, Bruce's mother is upside down and still in the car. She is barely conscious. Her face is cover in blood, some from Bruce as he was ejected from the car and from a big gash on her forehead where her head hit the steering wheel.

Bruce's mother hears someone walking towards her overturned car. She fights through the pain as she turns her head slightly to see who is coming.

Someone wearing black leather boots and a powder blue velvet dress steps into view by the driver's window.

Bruce's mother pleads for help in a shaky, painful voice. "H-h-help m-m-me."

A female hand with light blue fingernail polish reaches through the shattered driver's window and rips the seat belt from around Bruce's mother.

Free from her seat belt, Bruce's mother falls out of her seat. She moans in pain as she hits the ground with a loud thud.

The hand that freed Bruce's mother from her seat belt reaches in again, grabs Bruce's mother by an arm and pulls her out through the driver's side shattered window without any regards or concern for the injuries that Bruce's mother might have sustained.

Once out of the car, Bruce's mother is tossed onto the ice and snow-covered road as if she were some old dirty rag doll.

Bruce's mother struggles to open her eyes. She can barely make out who pulled her out of the car and tossed her onto the road.

Everything is a blur to Bruce's mother.

The woman that pulled Bruce's mother from the car is standing by the smashed, overturned car. She pulls the hood off her head. The woman is a younger Holly.

Holly walks over to Bruce's mother. She kicks some snow into the face of Bruce's mother.
"Hello, Madison." Holly says as she squats by Madison's blood covered head. Holly moves some hair away from Madison's eyes so that she may look into Madison's pain-stricken eyes.
Madison moans in pain.
Holly stands up. She turns and looks at Bruce lying in a snowbank. Holly then whistles softly.
Seconds later, something large is heard, smashing its way through the trees and thick foliage.
Frostbite steps out into the clearing by Bruce. He looks at Holly as if to look for her approval.
Holly gives a slight nod to Frostbite.
Frostbite in return bares his razor-sharp teeth, growls then picks up a bleeding and severely injured Bruce by one of his broken legs and holds him upside down.
A soft, painful moan escapes Bruce's bleeding lips. Barely conscious, he asks his mother for help. "Mom… Help me. I hurt."
Frostbite takes Bruce's other broken leg with his free hand so that Bruce's body is now dangling in front of him with Bruce's back facing him.
Frostbite smells Bruce's blood covered head. Then… without any kind of warning, Frostbite quickly snaps his powerful jaw closed around the back of Bruce's head. There is a loud cracking sound as Frostbite's teeth penetrate deep into Bruce's skull.
Bruce screams. His body violently convulses.
Frostbite growls with Bruce's head still in his mouth. Bruce's head is then ripped from his body as Frostbite pulls Bruce's broken legs apart in opposite direction like a wishbone being snapped in half.
Bruce's body is ripped in half, straight down the middle of his torso. Blood sprays everywhere as his entrails

drop in the snow.

The front of Frostbite is splattered and stained with Bruce's blood. Frostbite throws both halves of Bruce's body off to the side then takes Bruce's decapitated head that is still in his mouth and bites off a chunk of Bruce's head as if it were an apple. Frostbite discards the rest of Bruce's head as he chews and swallows the part of Bruce's head he bit off.

The chunk of Bruce's head in Frostbite's mouth makes a loud crunching sound as Frostbite's sharp teeth turns Bruce's brain and skull into bloody mush and bone fragments as he chews.

Frostbite swallows every last bit.

Holly turns to Madison. "Now your turn." Holly steps over Madison and disappears into a snow devil the suddenly appears out of nowhere.

Two white reindeer cows run out from the cover of the thick woods and trample Madison's limp body as they also disappear into the same snow devil that Holly disappeared into.

When Frostbite has gathered up the dead bodies of Bruce and Madison, he fallows his family.

Frostbite steps on the can of hickory honey ham, smashing it before he too disappears into the snow devil.

17

DEATH OF AN ALPHA

Later that night, after Gammy's shift at the local dinner has ended, she arrives at her house to find it quiet and dark in her house. Usually When Gammy comes home from work, Madison and Bruce are waiting to greet her.

"Maybe they've just gone out somewhere and shut the lights off on their way out." Gammy says to herself as she puts her car into park. She then shuts her car off and gets out. When Gammy reaches her front door, she unlocks the door and walks in, shutting the door behind her.

The first thing that Gammy notices in her house is that the only light is coming from the moon which is shining in through a window shade but even that isn't much light. She also notices that it's a bit chilly in the house as well.

Gammy thinks it's a little bit unusual. Madison knows she usually keeps some kind of night light on so she can see when she gets home at night. So, Madison has never turned off the lights.

And as far as there being no heat, Gammy doesn't like the cold whatsoever so, when it's cold out and she is away from the house, Gammy likes to keep the temperature of the house set at seventy-nine degrees so that when she comes home, it's nice and warm for her.

As Gammy makes her way through her dark and chilly house, she notices a slight cinnamon and pine aroma, something she has never smelt in her house before, at least at the same time that is.

Gammy finds a light switch on the wall and flips it on but the lights do not come on. She flips the light switch on a few more times but still, the lights do not come on.

On top of the lights not coming on, Gammy still smells the cinnamon and pine which is getting stronger as she makes her way to the back of her house.

As Gammy gets closer to the dining room in the back of the house, a strong scent of a dead fish and skunk slaps Gammy in her face.

The scent is so strong, Gammy can taste it in her mouth.

Gammy starts to feel sick. Her stomach turns and cramps up. She quickly covers her mouth as if to keep herself from throwing up.

Gammy dry heaves a few times then finally throws up a little in her mouth. She wants to spit the vomit out but not being able to see where a wastebasket is in the dark, Gammy takes out a balled-up tissue from her pocket, quickly opens it and then spits out the vomit into her tissue. When she is done, Gammy balls the tissue back up and returns it to her pocket.

The smell of the dead fish and skunk is so strong that it overpowers the cinnamon and pine that gammy was smelling and is only getting stronger as gammy makes her way through her house.

When Gammy reaches the living room, she looks around to see if she can see what smells so bad. But, because of it being so dark and unable to find a working light switch, Gammy cannot see a thing except for her Silver Queen Ann style floor cheval oval mirror which is in one of the corners on the far end of the living room.

A sliver of moon light has found its way through a window blind and is now illuminating Gammy's mirror which is starting to magically frost over, along the bottom and slowly working its way up along the sides of the mirror.

Gammy feels along one of the living room walls and finds a light switch. When she flips the switch, the lights still do not come on.

Puzzled as to why the lights won't turn on, Gammy takes a step into the dark living room.

Gammy hears two women giggling behind her. She quickly turns around and jumps back while screaming.

Prancer and Vixen slowly step out of the shadows, holding hands.

The twins are wearing their white gothic, leather trench coats that are closed and zipped up. The twins' white leather high platform boots make a tapping sound with each step they take as they walk across Gammy's wood floors.

Prancer is the first of the twins to speak. "Hello…"

Vixen finishes the sentence that Prancer started. "…Gammy."

"What the hell! Who the fuck are you guys and what are you doing in my house?" Gammy asks as she stands straight up. Gammy might be old but she is ready to defend herself against the trespassers if need be.

Prancer and Vixen continue to giggle as they back Gammy up into the living room.

"You're the last…" Vixen says with a mischievous smile.

Prancer has the same mischievous smile. "…of your pack."

"It's the alpha's turn to die." The twins say at the same time then giggle.

A low growl is heard coming from the same shadows that Prancer and Vixen stepped out of.

When Gammy reaches the middle of her living room, Frostbite growls again as he steps out from the shadows.

Because he is taller than the ceiling, Frostbite has to stand hunched over with his knees slightly bent. But even then, it still doesn't give Frostbite much room to walk.

The front of Frostbite is still stained with Bruce's blood.

Gammy stumbles backwards and falls on her ass as she screams at the site of the huge furry monster hunched over in her house.

Frostbite has got his arms at his side with each half of Bruce's body in each hand but because it's still too dark in the living room, Gammy is unable to see what Frostbite is holding in his hands.

Gammy quickly gets to her feet and stumbles back against her stone fireplace. She reaches for the mantle to keep herself from falling again and as she does, Gammy touches something lumpy, soft, and wet. She quickly let's go of what she touched.

Gammy gets her footing as best as she can and continues backing away from her intruders.

Gammy puts her hands up in front of her. "Please don't hurt me." Gammy begs.

Unknown to gammy, her mirror is now almost frosted over with ice crystals all over it.

Prancer and Vixen giggle at Gammy's words.

"We aren't the ones…" Prancer says with a mischievous smile.

Vixen finishes. "…who are going to hurt you."

The wins point to the mirror and say in unison, "Mother is."

As Gammy turns to looks at the mirror, Frostbite throws both halves of Bruce's body. One half of Bruce's body hits Gammy in the middle of her back while the other half takes Gammy's knees out, causing her to fall down. Her back side and legs are now covered in her grandson's blood.

Gammy screams as she crawls to the mirror.

A low, drawn out whistle is heard. Seconds later, candles that were placed throughout the house by Gammy's intruders, magically light.

The whistle stops when all the candles are lit.

There is now a soft warm glow to Gammy's living room.

Gammy leans back against her mirror and takes in the horrific site in her living room.

Right away, Gammy's eyes are drawn to the strangers in her house.

Gammy screams when she sees the huge furry monster standing next to two identical twins

Gammy slowly turns her head to her left and sees Madison or what's left of Madison, slumped over on the couch with what looks to be a slightly smaller, severed head with a big chunk taken out of it, sitting on her lap.

Because the face of the severed head is turned away from Gammy, she cannot see who it is.

Both of Madison's arms and legs have been broken and bent in directions they are not meant to be in. Madison's face is caved in with her eyeballs hanging out of their sockets by just their optic nerve.

Madison is also topless and missing her breasts.

Gammy's eyes and mouth widen as she covers her mouth with her bloody hands. She is in such shock that she cannot scream or say a word.

Gammy's attention now turns to the mantle above the fireplace.

Nailed to the mantle are Madison's severed breasts like stockings at Christmas time. Except that Madison's breasts aren't stuffed with tasty treats and toys. Her bloody breasts are overstuffed with coal.

Gammy then notices on the floor in front of the fireplace is what looks to be two bloody towels, twisted and mangles.

As the light from the candles flicker, Gammy squints to get a better look at the bloody towels.

Prancer and Vixen are giggling again.

Once Gammy realizes the towels in front of the fireplace are not towels, she loses it. "NO! NO! NO! NOT MY BABY!"

A soft, drawn-out whistle is heard again.

Gammy is crying hysterically as she continues to lean against her mirror.

The whistle stops.

Then… two hands with powder blue sleeves and white fur cuffs exit the ice-covered mirror and grabs onto Gammy's hair. The hands quickly pull Gammy into the mirror, headfirst.

Gammy kicks and screams.

Once Gammy has been pulled all the way into the mirror, the frost and ice on the mirror quickly vanishes, leaving no trace of what just happened.

Back at Christmas Village, sometime later.

An old, timeworn Holly is standing at her bedroom window, staring out at what used to be a winter wonderland as a homemade, black antique pillar candle lantern with a round glass covering and a decorative red and green plaid bow, that her husband made for her, long ago, burns on the windowsill beside her. She hopes that maybe one day her loving husband will see the light of the lantern and return to her.

Holly is wearing a powder blue, crushed velvet hooded robe with white fur around the hood, hemlines and cuffs.

Holly's hands are shaking ever so slightly as she reaches into one of her robe pockets to pull out her husband's white handkerchief with the letters "K.K" monogrammed on it.

It's been some time, but Holly remembers the last time her loving husband kissed her as if it were just a few minutes ago.

Holly closes her eyes.

She can feel a cold winter breeze of the North Pole blowing on her face as her husband's warm soft lips gently touch hers.

And then to watch her husband turn and slowly walk to his sleigh with his head hung low, she knew then that something was wrong but did nothing.

Holly truly believes that if she had stopped her husband from going out on his sleigh ride that fateful night or insisted that she go with him, then they would still be together today.

But for some reason unknown to her, she did nothing and it's a decision she regrets dearly.

Holly opens her tear-filled eyes and sniffles then wipes her eyes with her husband's monogrammed handkerchief. Afterwards, she returns the handkerchief to her robe pocket.

The aurora borealis dances across the night sky, twisting and curling like a well-orchestrated symphony of green lights.

Holly sniffles again as she now looks out onto her family's property and all the dark and abandon buildings on the property; the large barn that housed the reindeer and sleigh, a massive workshop that also had a post office in it, a bakery and sweet shop, elf housing that was home to 110,000 plus elves, a blacksmith, a doctor's office and a hot cocoa stand that her husband frequented quite often.

Holly thinks back to when the smell of freshly baked goods filled the air, mistletoe and colorful lights were stung everywhere.

There was a time when hundreds of Christmas trees scattered all over the Kringle property. Each tree was adorned with homemade decorations, colorful lights, and a star on top of each one.

Caroling and laughter could be heard everywhere. And the workshop... The workshop would be buzzing with all kinds of activity around the Christmas season.

Now, years after the death of Holly's husband, everything is dark and eerily silent.

There is no laughter or Christmas caroling. There is only sadness.

The once colorful lights are no more. Some of the strings of once colorful lights are pulled down in places.

There is no smell of freshly baked cookies in the air. There is only a cold, crisp winter breeze.

All the mistletoe has shriveled up and died.

The hundreds of Christmas trees are dead and stripped of their lights, decorations, and star.

The buzzing workshop is silent as well.

The beautiful cobblestone streets and sidewalks are now buried under cold wet snow.

The life, love, and family that Holly loved and cherished for so many years is gone. Her world is forever changed.

There is a light knock on the bedroom door.

Holly's eyes are red and puffy. She sniffles, wipes a tear away with a finger then, "Yes?"

The twins answer at the same time. "Your bath water is ready mother."

A minute or two later, a large, East Indian Rosewood door with roses carved into it opens into a large rectangular, dimly lit bathroom that resembles something out of a rustic, resort spa.

It's a bathroom that Holly's husband made for her as an anniversary gift.

The lights have been turned down and in their place, there are lit white candle sticks of various sizes placed around the bathroom.

Apple cider and cinnamon incense are burning around the bathroom. If you were to close your eyes and breathe in deeply through your nose, you'd think someone were holding a cup of hot apple cider and cinnamon in front of you.

There is also a hint of a metallic odor in the air.

Mosaic flagstones cover every inch of the bathroom floor. The walls on either side of the bathroom are covered in slate stone until you get to the vaulted ceiling, where it is then finished in maple planks and recessed lighting.

The bathroom is trimmed out in East Indian Rosewood.

As you walk further into the bathroom, there is a his and hers sink on either side. Both sinks are glass vessels with snowflakes etched into both of them and copper faucets. Both sinks rest on black onyx countertops with mahogany cabinetry underneath. There's also a black and copper, oval mirror hanging over each sink.

At the far end of the bathroom on the right, there's a sauna big enough to fit six people that is made out of cedar with a toilet across from it.

Just a little further down from the sauna is a sixty-five-gallon hammered copper pedestal bathtub.

On the right side of the copper tub is a homemade stool made out of mahogany and on the other side of the tub there are mosaic flagstone steps that lead up to a slate

covered fireplace with a fire burning in it. The top of the fireplace is peaked with rectangle slabs of flagstone.
There is a large window flanking each side of the fireplace's peaked roof.
The fireplace's mosaic flagstone hearth extends out, over the top of the copper bathtub.
On the left side of the fireplace, there's a stack of firewood and on the other side of the fireplace, there are various sizes of river rock placed there for no other reason other than for decoration and a covered wicker basket.
Holly slowly walks into her bathroom, gently shutting the door behind her.
She is still in her older, timeworn form.
Holly stops and sighs. Although she has stopped crying, her eyes are still swollen and bloodshot.
Holly continues to slowly walk further into her bathroom with her attention focused on what's in front of her.
One of Holly's hands trembles as it brushes up against her husband's side of the bathroom countertop.
While keeping her attention to what's in front of her, Holly notices out of the corner of her eye, her husband's rectangular reading glasses resting in the countertop.

    Holly has a flash back to when her husband would put on his reading glasses and read the names from his naughty and nice list to her while he took a hot bath and she was straddling the end of the bathtub while being tied up by several pieces of red, hemp rope that were tied in beautiful, intricate patterns.
    A rollie poly, jolly old man named Kris, wearing just a red velvet robe with white fur trim gently kisses his wife on her cheek then disrobes before getting into a hammered copper pedestal bathtub full of hot water.

He sits back in the bathtub, admiring his beautiful wife.
Kris has a pair of gold rectangular reading glasses in one hand and a large red leather-bound book with silver and gold trim and swirly font that reads, "Naughty and Nice".
Kris puts his reading glasses on and smiles at his wife. He clears his throat then opens the book.
Holly smiles back at her husband without saying a word.
Kris pauses for a moment as he scans the pages of his book then, "Becky Chapman, oh dear, it looks as if you've been a very naughty girl this year. Theresa Smach…" Kris pauses for a moment to collect his thoughts and clears his throat once more before continuing. "Such a nice young girl. Your kind loving heart will get you far in this world."
Kris reads off more names from his book. "Tabatha Hart, you've had many chances to change your ways, but you just seem to love making my naughty list every year." Kris slowly moves his head from side to side then reads off another name. "Oh Rex, my poor boy. What am I going to do about you?" Santa sighs then continues. "I see so much potential in you, but time and time again, you insist on bullying everyone around you" Santa takes off his glasses and rubs his eyes. He then puts his glasses back on. "I don't even think putting coal in your stocking this year will make a difference. You'll probably just terrorize the neighborhood and throw the coal at one of the other neighborhood kids."
Kris looks at his beautiful wife, disappointingly while moving his head from side to side.
Holly looks at her husband with a warm, supportive smile.
Kris pushes his reading glasses up onto his nose

then continues. "Jenna Chapman, such a lovely, determined young girl. I see you're still trying to find that list that'll get you to the happiest place on Earth."

Before closing his naughty or nice book, Kris reads one more name.

"Oh my. Naughty Nicky." The name, Nicky alone, is enough to make Kris blush. "And not just the normal naughty. You've been naughty in spades."

Kris closes his naughty or nice book and sets it off to the side of the bathtub. And then his reading glasses.

Water splashes out of the bathtub as Kris slowly positions his head between his wife's legs.

They lock eyes as Kris looks up at his wife from between her legs.

Holly knows what's coming next and she can't wait. The thought alone makes the hairs on her neck and arms stand on end. Her toes curl with excitement.

Holly closes her eyes and tips her head back as her husband slowly and passionately kisses her inner thighs, working his way to her Christmas cream pie.

Holly's arms are covered in goosebumps as her husband devours her Christmas cream pie.

Holly moans. "Oh Santa."

Present time.

Within a few more steps, Holly walks past her husband's red velvet suite that has been neatly hung up, never to be worn again by him.

It's been sometime since the death of Holly's husband, so his scent is long gone from his red velvet suite, but Holly can still smell the cold winter air that has blown through it many times as if he had just worn it.

Soon, Holly is walking past the sauna on one side and the toilet on the other.

Holly slowly shapeshifts into her younger, shapely

self. She is now swimming in her large, powder blue crushed velvet robe that was once snug against her larger, older self.

Holly lets the powder blue robe fall to the bathroom floor, leaving her naked and exposed.

It's not much further after that that Holly is standing in front of her copper pedestal bathtub that her husband hand made for her.

Holly stops in front of the tub. She looks at the bathtub's contents. Instead of being filled with water, the bathtub is filled with blood.

Holly closes her eyes and breathes deeply, taking in the aroma of the hot apple cider and cinnamon incense. Holly can also smell the hint of metallic coming from the blood in the bathtub.

Holly opens her eyes as she exhales.

She looks up at an old, naked, wrinkly woman who is suspended a couple feet over her bathtub by some matte finished chains that are bolted to the bathroom ceiling and then are fastened to a leg spreader which is then connected to the old woman's ankles by leather straps and handcuffs.

The old woman's arms have been brought back and connected to the leg spreader by more leather straps and handcuffs around her wrists.

The old woman is also wearing a black leather head harness with a ball gag in her mouth.

Another chain coming down from the ceiling is clasped to the top of the leather head harness and drawn taut, so the old woman's head is in an upward position, exposing her neck.

Small gator clips are attached to each one of the old woman's nipples with a small matte black chain connected to each gator clip. The chains connected to the gator clips are brought up between the old woman's crotch and attached to the leg spreader, preventing the old woman's saggy boobs from hanging down.

The gator clips are biting into the old woman's nipples, causing droplets of blood to fall into the bathtub of blood.

The old woman is barely conscious. She moans as she slowly moves her head to look at Holly.

"Hello, Doris. Or should I say... Gammy." Holly pauses for a moment. The sadness in Holly's face is replaced with anger. Her face is now hard and rigid with rage. "So, you're the fucking bitch who gave birth to the monster who took the only one I ever loved and cared for." Holly backhands Gammy so hard that Gammy spins around one hundred and eighty degrees. "HOW DARE YOU!"

Gammy spins back to her original position.

A rosy, red imprint of the back of Holly's hand is left on Gammy's upper cheek.

Holly takes the chains that are connected to Gammy's gator clips. She looks at the chains and leather that are suspending Gammy from the ceiling. "Before your mangy mutt took the life of my husband, we used to have a set up like this. I mean, it wasn't as crude of a set up as this, but it did the trick and provided me and my husband with a lot of toe-curling excitement."

Holly has a quick flashback.

A rollie poly, jolly old man named Kris has got his beautiful, old, timeworn wife lying on her belly in front of the roaring fireplace in their bathroom.

Kris is gently wrapping red hemp rope around his wife's neck then bringing the same rope around behind her so that he can tie her hands and arms behind her back.

He is taking great care not to cause his beautiful wife any unwanted pain as he restrains his wife with beautifully woven knots.

When he is finished, Kris then slowly and carefully

sits his wife up and positions her at the end of the bathtub so that she is straddling the end of the bathtub with her legs spread wide and on either side of the bathtub.

Holly moans with excitement.

Back to the present time.

Holly looks over at a small, covered wicker basket by the fireplace where her husband kept their red hemp rope.

Holly pauses for a moment then, "Among other reasons, do you know what I loved about my husband?" With a single tear rolling down her cheek, "My wonderful husband continued to love me over the years even with all my rolls, curves, gray hair and wrinkles. My husband loved me for who I was even though I was perfectly imperfect. And in return, I loved him for the same reason."

Holly gives the chains such a hard yank that the gator clips are ripped off Gammy's nipples.

Small pieces of Gammy's nipples are left in the pointed teeth of gator clips.

There is now a steady trickle of blood coming from where the gator clips were ripped off.

Blood from Gammy's nipples is added to the blood that's already in the bathtub.

Blood also drips from Gammy's mouth as she moans.

Holly steps back. She then slowly looks at Gammy's old, naked, wrinkled body.

Disgusted and enraged at the sight before her, Holly turns and walks to the steps leading up to the fireplace. When she reaches the fireplace, Holly walks over to one of the windows and peers out.

"Do you know, when I was a little girl, a pack of wolves killed my birth mom and dad?" Holly pauses for a second then continues. "A portly, jolly old man wearing a red velvet suit and his wife came along and saved me. By the time they arrived, there was nothing they could do for my mom and dad. The wolves had done their damage. The portly old man and his wife scared the wolves away then took me and the remains of my mom and dad with them home and raised me with their son as if I were their own."

Holly walks over to a stack of logs, picks up a couple pieces and puts them into the roaring fireplace.

Holly turns to face Gammy. "The old man and his wife didn't harm one hair on any of those wolves and because of that, that pack of wolves came back years later and took the life of my husband and caused the death of many of my friends and family members. Oh sure, it wasn't the same pack of wolves, but it was a pack of wolves none the less."

The only thing Gammy is able to do is moan in pain.

Holly slowly walks back down the steps until she reaches the side of her coper tub. Holly reaches down into one of her robe pockets, on the floor and pulls out a sharpened letter opener. "My husband used this very same letter opener to open hundreds of letters that he received from all the little boys and girls from around the world. And now, I'm going to use it to open you."

Holly looks at Gammy with an evil smile as she holds the sharpened letter opener. "I won't make the same mistake my husband's parents did. I took care of your pups, your male alpha and the rest of your pack and now…"
Holly pauses for a second then, "it's time to take care of the female alpha of the pack."

Gammy moans again.

"Don't worry though, you won't be alone in your time of death. This bathtub is filled with the blood of your pack. Oh sure, I mean some blood was lost in the process so, some water was added to the tub to make up for what was lost. The leather cuffs around your wrists, ankles, and the face mask that you're wearing are made from the hide of one of the members from your pack." Holly reaches up and taps the mask that Gammy is wearing. "You might know him as Morris. Oh, and the ball gag in your mouth... his scrotum." Holly chuckles.

So that she doesn't spill any of the blood that's in the bathtub, Holly slowly puts one leg into the tub while hanging onto the side of the bathtub, so she doesn't slip. With the letter opener in her hand, Holly then slides the rest of her naked body into the bathtub until she is submerged except for her head.

Holly enjoys the cold, thick, sticky blood all over her body. She breathes in the metallic odor of the blood that's in her copper bathtub.

Holly looks up at Gammy. "My husband was much like his father. He didn't have one violent bone in his body. If he were alive today and it was him that is here instead of me, he would have shown you mercy and let you go. That's just how he was." Holly stares up at Gammy in silence for what seems like minutes then, "But guess what? My husband isn't here. I AM!"

Holly quickly reaches up and draws the sharpened letter opener across Gammy's exposed neck.

The letter opener cuts through Gammy's neck like a hot knife through butter.

Gammy thrashes around.

Blood gushes out and splashes down onto Holly's face.

A sense of euphoria washes over Holly as she listens to Gammy's filleted throat making a gurgling sound while Gammy's blood cascades down onto Holly's face like some unholy rite of passage.

18

ARCTIC ENEMA

Years later.
11P.M. Holliday Mountain Ski Resort, Ellicottville, New York
Light from the winter moon is illuminating a fresh blanket of snow that has just fallen and covering everything as far as then eye can see.
Shadows from the trees dance in the moon light as a gentle winter breeze blows down through the ski slopes of Holliday Mountain Ski Resort.
Conrad steps out of the back door of his slope side cabin with only a pair of shorts on and a towel draped over his shoulder while his wife sleeps the night away.
Conrad makes a beeline for a bubbling and steaming hot tub. His bare feet are pale and ice cold by the time he reaches the hot tub.
Conrad hurries into the warmth of the hot tub as he drapes his towel over the side of the hot tub. He lets out a huge sigh of relief as he lowers himself into the bubbling hot tub.
The warm bubbling water sooths and warms Conrad's sore and chilled body.
Conrad looks around at his snow-covered surroundings. He then closes his eyes and rests his head on

the edge of the hot tub as he enjoys the warmth of the hot tub.

Conrad thinks about the last few days and the fun he's had with his wife and his church retreat.

It's been a while since Conrad has had this much fun.

Even though there is a chill in the air, the night is somewhat quiet and peaceful.

On top of hearing the bubbling hot tub, Conrad can also hear loud music and a party off in the distance.

Late night skiers can also be heard swooshing down one of Holliday Mountain's slopes.

Conrad's relaxation is short lived. As he takes in the cold winter air through his nose, a strong spicy-hot odor fills Conrad's nose, followed by the sharp refreshing smell of pine.

Conrad smiles from ear to ear. He remembers what happened the last time he smelled these two aromas together. And man… It was something every man dreams of.

Conrad quickly opens his eyes and instantly sits up in the hot tub. He quickly looks around while at the same time, enjoying the strong cinnamon and pine aroma that's grabbed onto Conrad's nose like a pair of vice grips.

The cinnamon and pine are so strong that Conrad can taste them both as he licks his lips, first sweet and spicy then a perfumy taste tickles his lips.

Conrad can hear the faint sound of jingle bells off in the distance.

Conrad turns his head and as he does, out of the corner of his eye, he sees what seems to be two white reindeer cows flying through the night sky, just above the tree line.

Conrad watches the reindeer with a wide-eyed expression as the reindeer slowly descend into the

glistening treetops until they disappear out of sight.
　　　The jingle bells stop.
　　　Conrad stands up in the hot tub with a flabbergasted look on his face. He doesn't know what to think. He rubs his eyes in disbelief. "What the…" The only time Conrad has ever seen flying reindeer was in the movies.
　　　A small crisp winter breeze blows the cinnamon and pine odor right into Conrad's face again. This time, it's even stronger.
　　　Conrad watches to see if the reindeer cows walk out of the grove of trees that they went down in.
　　　With it being so dark out, it's hard for Conrad to see anything within the grove of trees. But then after a few minutes, Conrad hears someone or something walking towards him from within the grove of trees where the reindeer went down in.
　　　The sound of jingle bells can be heard again. This time, the jingle bells are coming from within the grove of trees.
　　　First one reindeer cow steps into view and then the other.
　　　As the two reindeer step into view, they both shapeshift into two women, two women that go by the names of Prancer and Vixen.
　　　The twins still have their platinum blond pixie haircuts with the sides of Vixen's head still shaven.
　　　Prancer and Vixen take each other's hands, gently interlocking their fingers.
　　　Prancer is wearing skintight, white leather pants that look like they've been painted on with knee high white platform boots that buckle all the way up. Prancer is also wearing a white leather and lace corset that laces up and ties in the front. A white lace choker with a small silver jingle bell completes her outfit.
　　　Vixen has got a white lace bra and thong on with

white fishnet pantyhose that go all the way up to her upper thighs. There is also a white Christmas ribbon loosely wrapped around her upper body and pelvic area. Vixen is wearing white leather, platform boots that go to just below her knees and buckle all the way up. And like her sister, Vixen has got a white lace choker on with a small silver jingle bell on.

"Hello Conrad." The twins say at the same time with mischievous grins on both their faces.

Conrad is overwhelmed with Prancer and Vixen's beauty. "OH... MY... GOD!"

Oh sure, Prancer and Vixen's looks might have changed a bit, they're a little thinner with platinum blond pixie haircuts and smoky eye, but Conrad still remembers the first time he met the twins.

Conrad looks back at his cabin to make sure there are no signs of his wife then, without a word from his mouth, Conrad unties his shorts and lets them drop into the hot tub.

The twins shake a finger at Conrad while giggling. "Oh, no, no, no." The twins say at the same time.

"Not this time..." Prancer says.

"...silly boy. When we first met..." Vixen finishes her sister's sentence but then continues with her own.

"...it was your pleasure. But this time around..." Prancer says.

"...it's going to be our pleasure." The twins say at the same time.

At that moment, an odor so putrid that it makes Conrad gag, slaps him in his face like a wet towel.

Conrad feels hot air blowing down on the back of his neck. Thinking that it might be his wife, Conrad slowly and cautiously turns his head only to find that it's not his wife breathing down on his neck.

Standing behind Conrad and the hot tub is a nine-foot-tall furry beast with bone protrusions sticking out of him known as, Frostbite.

Conrad's eyes slowly follow Frostbite's massive body all the way up to his head.

As Conrad and Frostbite's eyes lock, Conrad hears his wife scream at the top of her lungs from inside their cabin.

Conrad's attention is quickly drawn to where his wife is screaming. He then looks back to the beast towering over him.

Frostbite's face wrinkles as he bears his sharp teeth and growls at Conrad.

Conrad screams as he tries to jump out of the hot tub.

Before Conrad can get even one foot out of the hot tub, Frostbite stops him with a large hand around Conrad's neck.

Frostbite's hand tightens around Conrad's neck as he forces Conrad back into the hot tub's water.

Conrad splashes around in the hot tub. He fights to break free from Frostbite's tight grip around his neck.

Conrad's screams have stopped. He now gasps for air as he claws and scratches at Frostbite's hand.

The twins' giggling has stopped. They are now watching in silence and with evil smiles as Conrad is being manhandled by Frostbite.

Frostbite takes a deep breath. He fills his lungs with the cold winter air around him and holds it in for a second or two then, slowly exhales into the hot tub.

The water in the hot tub gets cold then freezes over within seconds, turning into one big ice cube, trapping Conrad in the water from his knees down.

Frostbite let's go of Conrad's neck.

Conrad falls back, landing on his hands and naked ass.

As soon as Conrad's naked ass touches the frozen water, he stands right back up, as straight as he can, even though the lower half of his legs are frozen in the water.

The screaming in the cabin has stopped.

Conrad looks at his now silent cabin for a few seconds then quickly turns to the twins with so much rage that he forgets about the massive beast behind him. "IF YOU HARM A HAIR ON MY WIFE, I'M GOING TO FUCKING KILL YOU!"

Unmoved by Conrad's threatening words, the twins take a step towards Conrad while still holding each other's hand.

"Your words do not…" Prancer says with a mischievous smile.

"…scare us little man." Vixen finishes the sentence that her sister started.

The twins giggle then gaze lovingly at each other.

Vixen moves in closer to her sister.

Both sisters close their eyes as their lips touch. Bodily fluids are exchanged as they take turns sucking on one another's tongue.

Conrad watches the two women's display of affection towards one another. A small part Conrad wishes he were in the middle of the two women while another part of him wishes he were beating the hell out of them for what might have been happening to his wife in his cabin.

The twins eventually stop their kissing long enough to blow Conrad a kiss then turn and walk back into the grove of trees where they came from.

"HEY! WHERE IN THE HELL ARE THE TWO OF YOU GOING? GET ME THE FUCK OUT OF HERE! NOW!" Conrad hollers to the twins.

The Twins ignore Conrad and keep walking into the grove of trees until they can no longer be seen.

Prancer and Vixen's jingle bells can be heard as the

twins disappear into the darkness.

When Conrad feels the hot air on his neck and naked back along with the putrid stench of a skunk that just walked through a rotting fish market, it is then that Conrad remembers the beast that is behind him.

Conrad slowly turns his head around as much as he can. His eyes widen with fear as he sees the beast's face within inches from his.

Frostbite's face wrinkles and hardens as he bears his sharp, clenched teeth at Conrad.

Conrad quickly turns away from the beast and screams for help. He tries to leap out of the hot tub but soon remembers that he's trapped in the hot tub's frozen water. Conrad then uses his hands to try and pull himself out of the ice while he screams for his life.

Frostbite reaches down with one hand and touches the hot tub's frozen water.

The icy hot tub makes a cracking sound. Soon after, a thick, pointed icicle positioned between Conrad's legs, starts to slowly rise up from the ice in the hot tub.

Conrad quickly looks down between his legs when he hears the ice crack. He sees the pointed icicle slowly rising up towards his exposed crotch.

"WHAT THE FUCK!" Conrad yanks up on his legs in hopes that he might be able to break free from the ice. "COME ON, GET ME THE HELL OUT OF HERE!" Conrad pleads for help to whomever might be listening.

Conrad quickly looks behind him but to his surprise, the beast has silently disappeared into the night without so much of a trace of him ever being there.

Soon after, Conrad is thrashing around like some wild animal caught in a trap.

Conrad is still unable to break free from the ice.

As the thick, pointed icicle draws closer to Conrad's scrotum sack, Conrad cups his scrotum and penis and lifts them up and away from the point of the icicle. With his other hand, Conrad grabs the icicle and tries to unsuccessfully break it off.

The icicle continues to get closer to piercing Conrad. But now that Conrad has moved his scrotum and penis out of the way, the growing icicle is within inches of Conrad's taint.

Conrad screams as loud as he can as he violently yanks up on his legs, trying to break free.

Conrad is now hitting the side of the growing icicle until his hand starts to bleed.

The icicle finally breaks in half.

Conrad is so relieved that he lets go of his scrotum sack and penis and falls forward on his hands. He closes his eyes and lets out a huge sigh of relief, unaware that another pointed icicle has started to form on top of where the first icicle was broken off.

The ice in the hot tub begins to make a cracking sound again as the new pointed icicle continues to rise up between Conrad's legs.

Conrad hears the ice cracking and bolts up with a terrified look on his face. He looks down between his legs.

"GOD DAMN IT!" Conrad hollers as he moves his privates out of the way again and tries to break the icicle once more.

This time, the icicle doesn't break, it just keeps rising up towards a terrified Conrad.

Conrad screams and leans as far forward as he can with his hands on the ice in front of him so that he can get away from the growing icicle.

"Help me. Someone, please help me." Conrad whimpers.

As if by magic, the growing icicle bends and starts moving towards Conrad's asshole.

Conrad hears the ice crack but as he tries to see

what's causing the cracking sound, the ice under his hands quickly melts just enough for Conrad's hands to drop into the melted ice, all the way up to the middle of his forearms. The melted ice instantly freezes solid before Conrad has a chance to pull his hands free.

Conrad screams for help while wildly jerking his body around.

Conrad can feel the cold from the icicle as it gets closer to his asshole.

With his hands and legs frozen in the ice, the only thing Conrad can do to keep the icicle from piercing his asshole is to clench his ass cheeks and keep moving out of the way. But that only lasts for so long because within seconds, the icicle has found its way into the crack of Conrad's ass.

Conrad screams. He tightens his ass cheeks even more.

Because Conrad is moving and clenching his ass cheeks so tight, the icicle drives its way up into the side of one of Conrad's ass cheeks.

Conrad screams.

Blood flows from the wound in Conrad's ass cheek.

The icicle exits Conrad's ass cheek then enters his tight asshole and keeps going.

Conrad's screams sound just like a cat that just had its tail stepped on. His body stiffens as the icicle works its way up further into Conrad's body.

Blood flows from Conrad's mouth, nose, ears, and asshole.

Conrad stops his screaming. His body convulses.

The icicle stops when it exits Conrad's mouth, covered in blood.

19

MOUNTING THE HOLIDAY HERD

In the back room of a taxidermy workshop, an extremely overweight, middle-aged man named, William is sitting on a stool, hunched over a cluttered work bench, putting the finishing touches on a mounted pug.

William grabs a nearby cheeseburger from one of his favorite fast-food joints and takes a big bite out of it.

A big glob of ketchup squirts out from the cheeseburger and lands on William's shirt. "God damn it." William licks the ketchup off his shirt then puts the cheeseburger down and goes back to work on the pug while chewing the chunk of cheeseburger in his mouth.

William's shirt is sweat stained and riding up his hairy back, revealing his many hairy rolls. William's ass crack is also exposed and just as hairy as his back.

The taxidermy's back room is littered with all kinds of animals waiting to be stuffed and picked up by various customers; birds, dogs, cats, bears, mountain lions, bobcats, a beaver, and a few reindeer.

William leans to one side of the stool and lets a turd burner of a fart escape from his ass. He scratches his ass then grabs another big bite of his cheeseburger using the same hand that he scratched his ass with.

William then goes back to his work on the pug.

Jingle bells ring above the front door, alerting William of a customer walking into his shop.

William quickly lifts his head up and listens.

A strong cinnamon and pine odor fills the shop.

As William rolls his fat ass off his stool, he hollers to whom ever had just walked into his shop. "SORRY, I'M CLOSED FOR THE NIGHT!"

Eggnog is the last to walk into the taxidermy shop. He shuts the door behind him then joins the rest of his family as they make their way through the front of the taxidermy shop.

Just like in the backroom of the taxidermy shop, there are various species of animals in the front as well.

Covering one of the walls of the shop are heads of deer, big horn sheep, moose, and wild boar.

On the other side, the wall is covered with all kinds of fish; bass, walleye, pike, trout, and salmon to name a few.

As Holly and her family look around the taxidermy shop, they see whitetail deer, armadillos, a bobcat, a bison, a gray fox, a baboon, turtles of various sizes, a handful of squirls, an ostrich and bears of many sizes. There's even a reindeer cow pushed back into a dark corner of the shop.

Prancer and Vixen cannot believe their eyes. They start to cry at what they see.

With a disgusted look on his face, Eggnog looks around and, "This is so fucked up. Why would anyone want to kill and stuff a defenseless animal? I understand killing it for the food, but stuffing it and putting it on display?"

Holly explains to Eggnog without looking at him. "This is what the human race has come to. They no longer hunt just for food and clothing. Instead, they hunt for the sport."

The twins put their noses in the air and smell.

"They are here mother. I can smell them." The twins say at the same time.

From the backroom, William can hear talking from the front of his shop. He can't quite make out what is being said but he can hear the mumbling of people talking.

Meanwhile, sitting on a glass display case, Holly notices a small stuffed chipmunk up on its hind legs, by the cash register.

The chipmunk is holding a small sign that reads, "Please ring bell for service." And right next to the chipmunk is a sliver service bell with a black base.

Holly takes a moment to read the sign the chipmunk is holding then she taps the bell once. "DING!" Twice. "DING! DING!" Holly now taps the service bell repeatedly. "DING! DING! DING! DING!"

William rushes from behind the curtain that's separating the front of the shop from the back workroom.

William grabs Holly's hand that's ringing the bell. "Ease up on the fucking bell, lady. What? Are you impatient or something?"

Holly looks down in disbelief at the man's hand holding hers. "How dare he touch me." Holly says to herself.

There has been only one other man to ever touch Holly and that was her husband.

With a disgusted look on her face, Holly slowly looks up at the man who dares lay a hand on her.

Before Holly or William can say a word to one another, a hairy, leathery worn hand shoots up and around from the front of the display case and grabs onto William's hand.

"No one touches mother!" Eggnog stands up straight. His head and the top of his shoulder are the only

things about him that are visible to William.
    William is startled by Eggnog's sudden appearance, so he jumps back and yanks his hand away from Eggnog's grip. "WHOA! HOLY SHIT! Where in the fuck did you come from, little man?"
    Holly answers William instead of Eggnog. "I'm looking for some family members and I was told they were here." Holly's face goes hard and rigid.
    The glass display case that Holly has her hands on starts to slowly ice over.
    William's attention is focused on Holly, so he doesn't seem to notice the ice forming on his display case.
    William looks around at the mounted animals in his shop then back to Holly. "I don't know what you're talking about lady. It's just me and these fucking dead animals."
    Holly and William stare at each other without saying a word.
    Then, from one of the dark corners of the taxidermy shop, the twins let out ear piercing screams.
    Thinking they are in trouble, Eggnog rushes to Prancer and Vixen.
    When Eggnog reaches Prancer and Vixen, both women are crying hysterically by two mounted reindeer that are standing up.
    "WE FOUND DASHER AND BLITZEN!" Eggnog hollers to Holly.
    Both William and Holly quickly look in the direction of where the screams came from.
    William turns to look at Holly. He then catches a whiff of something dead. William turns around and as he does, the curtain separating the two rooms is violently torn down.
    Standing in the backroom is Frostbite who is hunched over just so that he can fit in the room. He has got three reindeer hides slung over his shoulder.

William jumps back against the glass display case. "HOLY SHIT!"

Frostbite puts one of his massive hands-on William's chest to prevent him from running off. Frostbite then lets the three reindeer hides fall on top of the glass display case as he leans into William to smell the side of his face. He smells the food on William's breath and starts to drool profusely.

Sleighbells on the three reindeer ring as they hit the glass display case.

Frostbite has eaten a lot of things in his lifetime but, a big juicy cheeseburger isn't one of them. He wonders if the scared fat man in front of him tastes as good as his breath smells.

Frostbite opens his mouth to take a chunk out of William's head.

William puts his hands up to his face to shield himself from Frostbite's mouth of sharp teeth.

Holly stops Frostbite. "No, not yet my friend. We're not done with this fucker."

The three reindeer still have their collars of sleighbells around their necks along with their name tags they were wearing when they last went out with Santa.

The reindeer's name tags are old and weathered but Holly is still able to make out the names on them. She reads each of the names on the tags to herself. "Comet, Cupid and Dancer." Tears stream down Holly's cheek. "There's one missing... Donner. Where is she?"

With fear in his eyes and afraid to move, "I don't know what you're talking about lady. I got those reindeer hides from a storage unit sale. There was no... Donner." William tells Holly.

Holly closes her eyes and takes a deep breath. As she exhales, a jagged piece of ice rises up from the glass display case, a foot into the air.

"Liar." Holly opens her eyes. She looks up at Frostbite.

With a shaky hand, William points to a far wall full of head mounts. "The only other reindeer I have is over there."

Holly looks to where William is pointing. When she sees the head mount of the reindeer hanging on the wall, she knows right away that it's Donner.

Without taking her eyes off Donner, "Where is the rest her body?" Holly asks as she slowly turns to William.

With a wide eyed expression frozen on his face, William answers Holly's question. "The customer only wanted the head mounted, so I threw the rest of the body in the trash a few days ago."

Holly quickly grabs onto William's ears and jerk his head back and down onto the jagged piece of ice until the tip of the jagged ice skewers William's right eye.

20

THE FINAL GOODBYE

Strong winds and a heavy snowfall are covering the North Pole as the first of three muffled church bells, the passing bell rings. The church bell echoes throughout the snow-covered trench maze.

An old, tired and time worn Holly fights the harsh winter elements as she and what's left of her family slowly walk down the many pathways of the trench maze, making their way to the Kringle mausoleum.
Any other day, Holly would have used her powers to control the winter elements and make it an easy trip to her family's mausoleum but not today.
The thousands of headstones that make up the trench maze of the dead are just about buried under all the snow. There are only a few headstones that are not buried under snow.
Even the eight-foot-tall nutcrackers that stand guard in the trench maze are just about buried under snow.

Finally, sheltered from the cold weather, in the Kringle's enormously domed, family mausoleum is an old and weathered Holly and her family; Frostbite, Eggnog, Prancer, Vixen, Pepper, Cupid, Twiggy, Snowman and a gingerbread named MOFO.

Each of them is wearing their finest clothing, well at least the ones that wear clothing that is.

Holly has got her white and gray hair neatly up in a bun, just like her husband liked it. Her gold, rectangular glasses are pushed up onto her nose. Holy is also dressed in her powder blue velvet dress.

The twins have got their white full length gothic trench coats on with their white leather, high platform boots.

Eggnog's sadden face is hidden by the hood of his brown monk's robe.

Pepper's oversized burgundy and white patchwork hooded parka is hiding most of what she is wearing underneath. Some of Pepper's red and white striped mini dress can still be seen. Pepper's red and white candy cane decorated white fur leg warmers are covering her legs and feet.

Pepper's crown of vines has been neatly placed on her red and white hair and adorned with fresh pinecones and pine needles from the Kringle Christmas tree farm, cranberries and freshly made candy canes

Cupid stands without her bow and arrows as a slight breeze blows the hemline of her low cut, sleeveless Victorian trumpet dress.

Twiggy's black gothic, trench coat is buttoned all the way up.

Even with the high winds and snowfall outside, the second of three church bells, the death knell can be heard from inside the mausoleum.

The interior of the Kringle mausoleum is decorated with East Indian Rosewood, copper accents and a white and black marble floor.

Hundreds of lit candles illuminate the interior of the mausoleum with a soft warm glow.
Shadows dance across hundreds niches filled with ashes of the Kringle family and close friends.
Holly and her family are gathered in front of six niches. Each one labeled with a different name; Dasher, Comet, Cupid, Donner, Blitzen, and Dancer.
Prancer and Vixen have dropped to their knees and are crying hysterically in each other's arms.
Frostbite and Snowman stand behind Holly and Cupid like two sentries.
Cupid is hiding her face in her hands as she cries.
Pepper sniffles as a teary-eyed Twiggy hands her a tissue.
With MOFO sitting on Eggnog's shoulder, Eggnog does his best to not let his hard exterior crack and let anyone see him cry as he casually wipes his tears away on his sleeves.
MOFO is somewhat new to the world, so he doesn't know what to make of all the weeping and crying. Quite frankly, he's kind of bored.
MOFO isn't used to just standing around, so he jumps off Eggnog's shoulder to the marble floor of the mausoleum. He lands with a grunt then runs off to do some exploring.
Holly does her best to keep her composure as a tear runs down her red puffy cheeks. She sniffles then wipes her tears away with a handkerchief that has the letters, "K.K." monogrammed on it in red and gold letters.

The lynch bell rings.

EPILOGUE

    Christmas Village as it was called by everyone at the North Pole was once a place filled with happiness and joy. Everyone knew everyone by their first name.
    Christmas Village was once a place that little boys and girls dreamed of. It was a place where their dreams and wishes came true.
    Now… years later, all is quiet in Christmas Village. Everyone is gone. The buildings that made up Christmas Village now stand dark, abandoned, and covered in snow, inside and out.
    Christmas Village is frozen in time, forever.
    It's been some time since Holly and her family have set foot in Christmas Village. They are but a distant memory to those who remember them.

    Elsewhere in the world, the miracle of life has just taken place.
    A crying, newborn baby boy is taken from his mother's womb, cleaned, and then gently placed in his mother's loving arms.
    The mother is crying as she kisses her newborn son on his forehead.
    A proud father watches the bond between mother and son being made.

    Back at Christmas Village, in an upstairs bedroom of the main living quarters, a leathery hand with hairy knuckles and black fingernails lifts the black venting cover off an antique pedestal candle lantern and lights a candle inside with a wooden match.
    Once the candle is lit, the leathery hand returns the

venting cover and then sets the lit lantern on a windowsill.

The decorative red and green plaid bow around the pedestal has seen better days as it is now starting to look tattered in places.

A beacon of light from the candle lantern cuts through the zero visibility that a blizzard is causing outside.

Minutes later, Eggnog exits the front door of the main living quarters with the help of an old, gnarled walking stick.

Eggnog shuts the door behind him.

The walking stick has a large white molar tooth recessed into the top of it.

Eggnog is wearing a thick, dark brown parka. The hood of the parka has been pulled over Eggnog's head with the drawstrings of the hood pulled and tied so the hood is closed in around Eggnog's face, so that only his eyes and cherry red nose are peering out, protecting most of his face from the frigid weather.

Eggnog is also wearing matching mittens and boots.

Eggnog looks up at the flickering light coming from the upstairs window of the main living quarters. He then watches the blizzard in front of him as if to be watching for something or someone.

As Eggnog takes a few steps away from the front door of the main living quarters, Frostbite steps out from around the main living quarters and joins Eggnog at his side.

Eggnog looks up at his huge friend and smiles. You can't tell because most of Eggnog's face is covered but the slight rise of his rosy cheeks gives his smile away.

Except for a few extra pounds and a bit more gray fur, Frostbite hasn't changed much over the years since Holly and everyone else left Christmas Village.

Eggnog and Frostbite's cold breath envelopes the front of their faces as the strong blizzardy winds blow.

"We have guests my old friend." Eggnog tells Frostbite.

Eggnog and Frostbite anxiously awaits to see who is making their way through the blizzard.

A soft drawn-out whistle is heard cutting through the wind and snow.

Eggnog's eyes widen with excitement as he recognizes who the whistle belongs to.

Frostbite takes off running into the blizzard where the whistle is coming from.

THE END!

Now we all know that it's never truly the end. It's just the prolonging of the inevitable.
So, to all, a sleepless night for I will see each and every one of you real soon.

-Holly

BONUS MATERIAL
Everything That Went into Writing Kringle, Severed Bloodline

Hello my twisted readers. I hope you've enjoyed the journey through another one of my many twisted and disturbing worlds, this one being Kringle, Severed Bloodline.

If you've enjoyed reading Kringle, Severed Bloodline, please go back to where you purchased Kringle, Severed Bloodline and leave a review, letting everyone know what you thought of the story. Or, if Kringle, Severed Bloodline was a gift from a friend, family member or a loved one, please go onto any and all social media sites and leave a review there.

Oh, wait... don't close Kringle, Severed Bloodline's cover just yet. Kringle, Severed Bloodline's journey isn't quite over.

Normally, after I've finished writing a story and it's gone to print, I usually throw out all my notes, thoughts and any discarded parts of the story that I did not use. Not this time though. This time, I'm doing something different.

I've decided to keep everything and include a special section called Bonus Material so you can see just what went into Writing Kringle, Severed Bloodline.

Some of you might think all this extra stuff is nonsense and unnecessary and then again, some of you might find it just as enjoyable as the story. Plus... If I decide to write a third Kringle (Anything is possible), I have all of this to look back on instead of trying to remember it all.

    In the following bonus material, you'll find my notes, character outlines and wardrobe, a couple discarded chapters that would have normally gone into the garbage, a list of music I listened to while writing Kringle, Severed Bloodline and maybe a few other tid bits that went into bringing my newest creation to life.

    I hope you enjoy the bonus material just as much as the story.

FACTS ABOUT KRINGLE, SEVERED BLOODLINE

Before deciding on Severed Bloodline as Kringle 2's subtitle, there were two other subtitles, Ghosts of Christmas Past and Ghosts of Christmas Future.

The scene where Holly's birth parents were killed by the pack of wolves was originally supposed to be a grizzly bear instead of the wolves. But as the story went on, I thought it would be better if it were a pack of wolves.

Most of Kringle, Severed Bloodline was written on my fifteen-minute coffee breaks and my half hour lunch breaks at work and anywhere in between while taking notes on my phone.

Kringle, Severed Bloodline was originally supposed to be out on Christmas 2020 but because of unforeseen circumstance, that release date never happened.
Then came the new release date for Kringle, Severed Bloodline, Christmas of 2021 but again, that never happened.
As the saying goes, "The third time is a charm." So, here in 2023, you're finally reading, Kringle, Severed Bloodline.

When it came time to decide on a name for the main gingerbread man character, I had three names; Motherfucker or MOFO for short, Oliver and Mr. Peabody.

The idea for Christmas Village's burial grounds or the trench maze as it's called, came from Lindsey Stirling's video, Crystallize.

The death of Darnel in Chocolatey Goodness was inspired by a roll of industrial plastic wrap that I use at my day job.

The idea and look for Frostbite came from the combination of two fictional characters; Doom from Superman and the Yetis from the movie, The Mummy: Tomb of the Dragon Emperor.

The idea for the hair in Darnel's cereal in Chocolatey Goodness didn't just happen. My wife was kind of the inspiration for that one. Anything that has to do with a hair in her or someone's mouth will cause my wife to gag.

I always tend to put a little bit of truth or a small part of my life into everything that I write.
The chapter, Coach Stall's Emasculation is evident of that.
I won't say what part of that chapter is true but my family and maybe a friend or two will know what the chapter is in regards to.
I will say this though, some of the dialogue in the chapter, Coach Stall's Emasculation is based after true events.

The Panthers football team in the chapter, Coach Stall's Emasculation was kind of a nod to my old high school, Pioneer Central High School. Our mascot was a panther.

What's the deal with the hickory honey ham in a can in chapter 6, Severed Bloodline? Well, it's nod (An Easter egg if you will.) to one of my favorite Christmas movies, Christmas with the Kranks. If you've seen the movie then you'll know the similarities with what happens to the hickory honey ham in the movie and in Kringle, Severed Bloodline.

Another one of my all-time favorite Christmas movies is National Lampoon's Christmas Vacation. In the chapter, Chocolaty Goodness, you'll find a small but subtle Easter egg (When Darnel pushes aside his Aunt "B's" green Jell-O mold.) that has to do with National Lampoon's Christmas Vacation.

For those who don't know, Aunt Bethany brought a green Jell-O mole to Clark Griswold's house the Christmas.

Every author, sometime in their life wants or dreams about having their books made into movies and who they would like to see portray their characters.

Me, I'm no different. My ultimate goal for my books is to see them up on the big screen.

If either of the Kringle books were to be made into a movie and I was given the power to cast the characters for it, the following list of names is who I would love to play the main characters in either of the Kringle books.

Holly Kringle – *Taylor Swift*
Eggnog – *Peter Dinklage*
Frostbite – *The Big Show* from the WWF
Prancer & Vixen – *Evanna Lynch*, but as I started to write Kringle, Severed Bloodline and the twins evolved and changed, so did Who I envisioned playing them. In Kringle, Severed Bloodline, the twins would be played by *@astarithy*
Cupid / Genevieve – *Diana Bastet @bastet_diana*
Snowman – I haven't quite figured him out yet.
Mr. Heat – *Danny Devito*
Pepper – *Amy Adams*

Twiggy – All I have is her first name and where she can be found on Instagram. *Theresa @theresafractale*

THE MUSIC BEHIND KRINGLE, SEVERED BLOODLINE

    The music I listened to while writing Kringle, Severed Bloodline had a big part in triggering the inspiration for some or all the things that took place in Kringle, Severed Bloodline.
    When it came to the music that I listened to while writing Kringle, Severed Bloodline it wasn't necessarily all the lyrics of a song that was the inspiration. Some of the things that took place in Kringle, Severed Bloodline were inspired by the beat of a certain song or maybe just one word of a song.
    The following list of songs, believe it or not, is what I listened to while writing Kringle, Severed Bloodline.

Crystallize by Lindsey Stirling
Carol of The Bells by Lindsey Stirling
Dance of The Sugar Plum Fairy by Lindsey Stirling
Friendship by Pascal Letoublon
In The Air Tonight by Phil Collins
Watermelon Sugar by Harry Styles
Cry Little Sitter from the Lost Boys Soundtrack
Do I Wanna Know by Arctic Monkeys
Hypnotize by Biggie Smalls
Party Up (Up In Here) My Mind by DMX
Psycho Killer by Talking Heads
In My Mind by Dynoro & Gigi D'Agostino
Bring Me To Life by Evenescence
What I've Done by Linkin Park
Wash It All Away by Five Finger Death Punch
Pony by Ginuwine
Love Me Like You Do by Ellie Goulding
You Dropped The Bomb On Me by The Gap Band

Turn Down For What by DJ Snake & Lil Jon
Salt Shaker by Ying Yang Twins (featuring Lil Jon & The East Side Boyz)
Lily Was Here by David Stewart & Candy Dulfer
Unstoppable by Sia
Lose Yourself by Eminem
Thriller by Michael Jackson
Voodoo by Godsmack
Down With The Sickness by Disturbed
Frozen by Madonna
River by Bishop Briggs
Little Drummer Boy by for King & Country (Live from Phoenix version)
Bananza (Belly Dancer) by Akon
Boom by Tiesto & Sevenn

When I was a kid and I listened to music, I listened to it because I liked it. I liked how it sounded and I liked the mood it put me in.

I enjoyed the music.

One thing I never did was sit and listen to a song so much that I was dissecting it to the point where I was finding some reason why it might be offensive.

If I didn't like a song for whatever reason, I just simply didn't listen to it, plain and simple.

Over time, this has changed though, at least with other people.

I guess some people have nothing better to do because in 2018, a handful of Christmas songs were found to be offensive to some people. So, some Christmas song were banned from being played on the radio.

The following list is a few of those songs and why they were found to be offensive.

As a way to show my love for the Christmas songs that were banned, I've cleverly written them into Kringle, Severed Bloodline by way of little subliminal "Easter Eggs".

I'm not going to tell you where they are in the story because there's quite a bit so, I'll leave it up to you to find them.

I Saw Mommy Kissing Santa Claus: *subjecting minors to softcore porn*

The Christmas Song: *cultural appropriation*

Holly Jolly Christmas: *unwanted advances*

White Christmas: *racist*

Santa Claus is Coming to Town: *peeping tom, stalker*

The Most Wonderful Time of The Year: *forced to hide depression*

Rudolph The Red Nosed Reindeer: *bullying*

It's Beginning to Look A Lot Like Christmas: *forced gender specific gifts*

Santa Baby: *gold digger, blackmail*

Frosty The Snowman: *sexist*

Do You Hear What I Hear: *blatant disregard for the hearing impaired*

Jingle Bell Rock: *animal abuse*

Mistletoe and Holly: *overeating, folks stealing a kiss or two*

Winter Wonderland: *forced partnership*

CHARACTER OUTLINE AND WARDROBE

Holly Virtanen Kringle (old, wrinkled and timeworn)

Age: Unknown

44" chest   39" waist   60" hips

Height: 5' 7"

Eye: blue (has a twinkle in them)

Wears gold, rectangular glasses.

Hair: white with streaks of gray
    The older Holly likes to keep her hair up in a bun, the way her husband, Kris loved it. Although her hair can get quite disheveled at times.

Holly Virtanen Kringle (when she is in her younger form)

34" chest   23 1/2" waist   36" hips

Height: 5' 10"   Weight: 121lbs.

Eyes: Ice blue
    When Holly is sexually aroused, her pupils will dilate and as she reaches her climax, her eyes will cloud over.

Long blond hair with dark roots. She likes to wear a tight French braid going down the back of her head with a tight water fall braid on either side of the French braid. Holly also has two French braids on either side of her head, around her temple area.

Wears powder blue fingernail and toenail polish.

Place of birth: Finland

Holly talks with a slight finish accent that has over the years become watered down the more time she spends away from her homeland.

She smells like hot apple cider with a hint of cinnamon.

Mother: Lavia Latvala (from Finland)

Father: Igor Virtanen

Holly was eight years old when her birth parents were killed by a pack of wolves.

Husband: Kris Kringle (deceased)

No biological children.

If nearby, Holly's victims will first hear a soft drawn-out whistle. The temperature will also drop.

Holly can travel from place to place and over long distances by way of snow devils. She can also open up ice portals by just freezing any smooth surface. She has also been known to use her husband's sleigh, the Nutcracker from time to time.

Holly has the ability to control the winter elements, an ability she got from both her mother and father.

Holly is fast and strong.

Holly can also shapeshift from her older timeworn self into a younger version of herself.

Holly's wardrobe

#1

Satin white gloves.

Powder blue, velvet dress with a zipper back and white fur edging on her collar, cuffs, hemline and center front.

The dress has a powder blue, crushed velvet skirt inset with gold embroidery at the hemline.

Powder blue velvet capelet has white fur edging with embroidery at the front edges of the crushed powder blue hood.

Her cape fastens at the neck with two white cords that have pom-poms on either end.

Her black leather belt has an antique gold buckle.

Holly wears a pair of glossy black Victorian boots that lace up the front.

#2

Holly also wears her traditional red velvet dress in the beginning of the story.

Eggnog

4' 5" Tall

Brown eyes

Eggnog is bald except for a goatee and hair covering his whole body. (Brown)

Eggnog likes to wear a brown monk's robe with a small magical pouch attached to his waist cord. The pouch can carry anything Eggnog wishes.

He walks with a slight wobble.

Eggnog's face is wrinkly and looks almost leathery.

He has a raspy sounding voice.

He teeth have also been sharpened to points.

Eggnog likes to collect human teeth and fashion necklaces out of them that he wears from time to time.

Eggnog's lineage on his mother's side of the family is said to date back all the way to the Paleolithic Era. There is no written records or any kind of proof of this, only the stories passed down through time.

If the stories are true, this would explain the excessive body hair and height difference between Eggnog and the rest of the elves that used to exist in Christmas Village.

Vixen

Age: Unknown

Tight hourglass figure

34" chest   26" waist   34" hips

Height: 5' 7" human form   6' 2" reindeer form

Weight: 125lbs. human form   308lbs. reindeer form

Long platinum blond hair in the beginning of the story then she has a pixie cut with the sides shaved for the rest of Kringle, Severed Bloodline.

Smokey green eyes with thin black eyebrows.

Pale complexion.

Black lipstick, fingernails and toenails.

Vixen has a slight cinnamon aroma to her that gets stronger when she gets excited or sexually aroused.

Words used to describe what Vixen can smell like at times; spicy-hot, sweet, warm and smoky

When Vixen is around her sister, they start and finish each other's sentences.

Vixen is Prancer's identical twin sister.

Vixen feels and experiences all of Prancer's pain and emotions.

Vixen's pubic area is totally shaven with a colored tattoo of a mistletoe just above her crotch.

Vixen is able to shapeshift into a reindeer cow.

She is extremely strong and fast in both her human and reindeer form.

Vixen likes to flirt but when it comes to satisfying her sexual needs, she turns to her sister.

Vixen has the ability to fly when in reindeer form.

She can also leap great distances while in both human and reindeer form.

The cinnamon odor that Vixen gives off can be quite euphoric at times. It can put anyone around her into a dream like state if the odor is strong enough

Vixen's wardrobe

#1

White lace bra and a thong to match.

White fishnet pantyhose that go to Vixen's upper thighs.

Thin white Christmas ribbon that's wrapped around Vixen's upper body and pelvic area.

White leather high, platform boots that go to just below Vixen's knees and buckle all the way up.

#2

White full length gothic trench coat with a flare skirt design and black satin lining.

The trench coat zips closed and has metal buttons that detail the front of the coat and the cuffs.

The trench coat also has slash pockets on the sides.

White leather high, platform boots that go to just below her knees and buckle all the way up.

#3

Eskimo styled, stretch crushed brown velvet skirt that ends a few inches below Vixen's crotch.

The skirt has an attached oversized hood with pom-pom

ties.

The hood, cuffs and hemline of the skirt are trimmed in white fur.

The front of the skirt has a zipper that unzips down to Vixen's bellybutton.

White mittens cover her hands.

Vixen wears knee high white boots trimmed with white fur and lace all the way up.

#4

White suede boots with white fur lining and an oversized silver knitted scarf.

Prancer

Thin, tight hourglass figure

34" chest   26" waist   34" hips

Height: 5' 7" human form   6' 2" reindeer form

Weight: 125lbs. human form   308lbs. reindeer form

Long platinum blond hair in the beginning of the story then she has a pixie cut for the rest of Kringle, Severed Bloodline, thanks to Mr. Heat.

Smokey green eyes with thin black eyebrows.

Pale complexion

Black lipstick, fingernails and toenails

Age: Unknown

Prancer has a slight pine aroma to her that gets stronger when she gets excited or sexually aroused.

Words to describe the odor that Prancer can give off at times; sweet, spicey, warm, clean and refreshing.

When Prancer is around Vixen, they both start and finish each other's sentences.

Prancer is Vixen's identical twin sister.

Prancer can feel and experience Vixen's pain and emotions.

Prancer's pubic area is totally shaven and has a colored tattoo of a mistletoe just above her crotch.

Prancer is able to shapeshift into a reindeer cow.

Prancer is extremely strong and fast in both her human and reindeer form.

Prancer has the ability to fly when in reindeer form.

She can also leap great distances while in both human and reindeer form.

Like her sister, Prancer likes to flirt but when it comes to satisfying her sexual needs, Prancer turns to her sister.

The pine odor that Prancer gives off can be quite euphoric at times. It can put anyone around her into a dream like state if the odor is strong enough.

Prancer's wardrobe

#1

A white leather and lace corset that laces up and ties in the front.

Skintight, white leather pants that look like they've been painted on. Rumor has it Prancer's leather pants are made from human skin.

Knee high, white platform boots that buckle all the way up.

#2

White full length gothic trench coat with a flare skirt design and black satin lining.

The trench coat zips closed and has metal buttons that detail the front of the coat and the cuffs.

The trench coat also has slash pockets on the sides.

White leather high, platform boots that go to just below her knees and buckle all the way up.

#3

Eskimo styled, stretch crushed brown velvet skirt that ends a few inches below Prancer's crotch.

The skirt has an attached oversized hood with pom-pom ties.

The hood, cuffs and hemline of the skirt are trimmed in

white fur.

The front of the skirt has a zipper that unzips down to Prancer's bellybutton.

White mittens cover her hands.

Prancer wears knee high white boots trimmed with white fur and lace all the way up.

#4

White suede boots with white fur lining and an oversized silver knitted scarf.

Mr. Heat

Real name unknown.

Age: Unknown

Height: 5'   Weight: 290lbs.

Eyes: blue

Hair: Bright, fiery red that sticks up everywhere. Mr. Heat's hair resembles a raging bonfire.

Body markings: Freckles on upper cheeks and nose.

Mr. Heat is short and stout.

Pale complexion. His face turns a shade of red when angered.

Mr. Heat is short tempered and easily angered.

Has the power to control fire.

Smells like sulfur.

Mr. Heat supposably has a brother named Snow.

Mr. Heat likes to wear black and white pin striped suites.

Frostbite

A male Yeti   Age: Unknown

Height: 9'   Weight: 16,000lbs.

Eyes: Ice blue   Skin color: Grayish purple

Frostbite is covered in white and gray fur from his head to his feet. The only places that do not have fur is his face, hands, feet and pectoral area.

Frostbite's ears are pointed.

He has sharp bone spikes protruding from the top of his shoulders, left elbow, right forearm, both knees and the knuckles on his hands.

Frostbite's thick skin and fur insulate his body from the harsh winds and extreme cold weather at the North Pole, Christmas Village.

Rough padding on the bottom of Frostbite's feet gives him the traction needed to stand, walk and run on ice without slipping or falling.

Frostbite carries a neurotoxin in his bloodstream and his other bodily fluids that will paralyze anyone that it comes in contact with.

Place of birth: Somewhere in the Himalayan Mountains

Smells like a dead skunk in a rotting fish market.

Frostbite's strength and speed are unmeasurable.

He has the ability to freeze anything he wishes, faster than liquid nitrogen. All he has to do is breathe on it.

Frostbite has a scar on his left eyelid and upper lip that was caused by a cattle prod when he was little (see Kringle, A Twisted Christmas Tale).

When Frostbite was younger, Holly saved him from a group of hunters who slaughtered his family. And now because of Holly's kindness, there is an unbreakable connection between Holly and Frostbite.

The rescue of Frostbite in Kringle, A Twisted Christmas Tale by Holly and some of her family, took place sometime before the events of the sickness in Kringle, Severed Bloodline. It was a time when Santa was still alive.

Holly didn't include her husband in the rescue of Frostbite because she knew her husband would have mercy on the hunters who killed Frostbite's family.
    It doesn't matter how evil someone is or what they have done, Santa would never harm a hair on anyone's head, man or beast.

Holly loves and supports everything that her husband believes in with all her heart except for when it comes to the inexcusable slaughter of wildlife or when it suits her needs.

That's why Holly chose to include only Eggnog, Prancer, and Vixen in Frostbite's rescue.

Twiggy / Easter Bunny

Hair: Jet black that goes to the middle of her back. Twiggy likes to keep her hair slicked back into a high ponytail. The hair of the ponytail is teased and wavy.

Height: 5' 8"   Weight: Unknown

Bust: 42" D   Waist: 26"   Hips: 35"

Eyes: turquoise blue

Twiggy's eyes are upturned.

Skin color: Brown when she is in her human form. When Twiggy is in her rabbit form, she is black and tan in color.

When in rabbit form, Twiggy's fur is slick and glossy.

Twiggy has the ability to shapeshift into a 6lb. black tan rabbit.

Slender built when in human form.

Inquisitive, intelligent and tactile.

She wears black lipstick and black eyeliner with the same color on her fingernails and toenails.

Place of birth: England

Twiggy twitches her nose when she is stressed or hot.

Twiggy has a small circular scar on the upper part of her left calf that she got from a hunter's bullet.

As a rabbit, Twiggy once had a lifetime partner named Peter Cottontail and together they had five kits (baby rabbits).

The death of Twiggy's husband, kits, and her rescue took place after Santa's death, sometime just after the sickness.

Twiggy's wardrobe

Black lace bra.

Black leather, tie back corset with white stitching and an attached black sheer corset skirt that is just about see through.

Black leather bracers with an elaborate Celtic cutout design in them.

Twiggy also wears a full length, black gothic trench coat that has a flared skirt.

Genevieve / Cupid

Height: 4' 11"   Weight: 94lbs.

Bust: 34"   Waist: 22"   Hips: 34"

Hair color: Jet black   Hair style: Dreadlocks, long

Left-handed

Born in 1793   Place of birth: London

Genevieve was born into an aristocrat family. Her father was a well-known businessman in London.

She was 18 when she was killed with her boyfriend, Abraham, by her father. (See Kringle, A Twisted Christmas Tale)

Genevieve is a contortionist.

She likes to wear loose fitting clothing and ruby red thongs.

Genevieve is a skilled archer with a long bow.

She uses an elaborately decorated, wooden longbow made out of white oak. 64" long

As Cupid, Genevieve loves to go bare foot most or all of the time.

Genevieve's wardrobe

Genevieve is partial to a low-cut white, medieval sleeveless trumpet Victorian dress with vintage lace mesh.

White Lolita bloomers with layered ruffles, lace trim and bow ribbons

Genevieve wears an all-in-one bracer and bow glove on her right hand. The bracer and bow glove are made of soft white leather and ruby red laces.

Abraham / Snowman

Year born: 1791   Place of birth: London

Born into the poorest of working class of hat makers.

Hair: Red   Eyes: Brown

Tall and slender

Body markings: Freckles on upper cheeks and nose.

Abraham was twenty years old when he was killed with his girlfriend, Genevieve. (See Kringle, A Twisted Christmas Tale)

As Snowman, he is six foot tall but can get bigger.

As Snowman, he rarely talks. If anything, it's just a handful of words.

The only article of clothing that is consistent with Snowman is his old, black silk top hat that he was wearing when he was killed.

Peppermint / Pepper

Age: Unknown

Eyes: Blue   Height: 5'   Weight: 98lbs.

Hair: Red with white streaks.

Place of birth: Germany

Hair style: A little longer than Pepper's shoulders. Straight with a loose braid on either side of her head.

Pale complexion with rosy, red cheeks.

Body markings: Some freckles on her upper cheeks and nose.

Wears red lipstick.

Pepper has a round face with prominent cheek bones and a small button nose.

Pepper talks with a slight German accent.

Pepper has been known to taste and smell like a peppermint candy cane.

For a woman of her size and stature, Pepper has no fear. She will stand toe to toe with anyone, man or beast who gets in her way.

When Pepper is aroused, fearful, startled, stimulated or excited in any way, her hair will stand on end.

Pepper's wardrobe

#1

Red and white striped, long sleeve mini dress with an attached hood and white fur trim around the hood, wrists and skirt line.

The mini dress zips up in the front. The dress also has a thick black belt with a silver buckle and double grommets.

Knee high white fur leg warmers with red and white striped ties with a pom-pom on the end of each tie.

Red and white striped candy canes decorate the front and back of the leg warmers.

#2

Pepper also wears an over-sized hooded parka over coat with a stitched burgundy and white patchwork pattern.

There is large white fur trim around the hood, zipper area, wrists and inside of the coat.

#3

Pepper on occasion will wear a crown made from vines and adorned with pinecones, pine needles, cranberries, and candy canes.

Motherfucker or MOFO (For short)

Height: 6"   Width from arm to arm: 5 ½ inches.

Eyes: two round white circles made from royal icing.

White royal icing is also used for his mouth and the squiggly lines on his wrists and ankles.

White and red royal icing is used for his bowtie.

Red royal icing is used for the three circles going down the front of his body.

The color of the royal icing can be changed up to change MOFO's expressions and how he is decorated to suite his needs and wants.

The color of MOFO's gingerbread body is maroon.

MOFO is vulgar and has no filter.

For a somewhat brittle cookie, MOFO has no fear.

MOFO was brought to life by a lot of TLC from Pepper and the blood from Mr. Heat.

MOFO's weight is unknown but he does have a large round potbelly. He is also somewhat round and thick.

MOFO talks with a high pitched voice.

Charlie in the box

Charlie is a small jack-in-the-box clown that has got powder blue hair that's wild and windblown even though he hasn't been out in the wind.

Charlie has a white face with a big powder blue nose and a big powder blue smile to match his hair color. He also has black diamonds painted over both of his eyes.

Charlies clothes consists of just a baggy long sleeved shirt that's white with black and powder blue circles. He also has a black bow tie with small powder blue circles all over it. Small white cotton gloves cover Charlie's hands.

The dimensions of Charlie's metal prison is 5.5 x 5.5 x 5.5

Charlie's life as a jack-in-the-box began in the Victorian Era. Back then he had a totally different color scheme, and his box prison was made out of wood. Over time though, his color and the box that he is confined to has been changed too many times to remember. Charlie is now locked away in a metal prison.

In Kringle, Severed Bloodline, Charlie's metal prison has a snowy winter wonderland scene painted on it, complete with Santa being pulled in his sleigh by his eight reindeer. There's also silver and gold trim all around Charlie's metal prison.

Charlie has a cynical laugh.

Nester

Nester is a kiang donkey from Tibet who was rescued / set free in Kringle, A Twisted Christmas Tale by the Kringle family.

Height: 52" at the withers   Length: 72"   Weight: 770lbs.

Its tail is 13"

Nester has a rich chestnut colored coat during the winter months and changes to a sleek reddish brown in the late summer.

Nester has a short black mane.

Even though Nester is friendly with the whole Kringle family, he seems to have a stronger connection to the twins.

THE HAND FAMILY TREE

Morris Hand married Doris "McAdams:" Hand (Gammy). Together, they had one son, Napoleon (died in Kringle, A Twisted Christmas Tale).

It wasn't too long after Morris' brother, Robert died that Morris found out that his wife and brother were having an affair for the longest time even though Robert was married (see Natalie).

Morris also found out that Napoleon wasn't his son. Napoleon was the love child of Natalie and Robert.

Morris stayed with his wife and Napoleon to try and work things out but it tore Morris apart every time he looked at his wife and the child he thought was his.

Unable to forgive and forget what his wife did to him, Morris walked out on Natalie and lived a sheltered life for years after.

Unknown to his family, Morris died of a massive heart attack and was later taken to the morgue at Tranquil Hospital.

Doris "McAdams" Hand (Gammy) (see Morris Hand)

Napoleon Hand married Caroline "Murphy" Hand (she died in Kringle, A Twisted Christmas Tale).

Together, they had three daughters; Jamie, Madison and Mandy (Mandy died in Kringle, A Twisted Christmas Tale).

Caroline Hand (see Napoleon Hand)

Jamie "Hand" Coder married Brian Coder. They had no children.

Brian Coder (see Jamie Hand)

Madison Hand never married but she at one time had a boyfriend whose name was William Jay.
    Together, they had one son, Bruce.

William Jay is a deadbeat father / junkie, living in New York City.
    William never married, but he did date Madison Hand for a brief time.
    Together, they had a son, Bruce.
    When Madison told William that she was pregnant with his child, he denied that it was his and insisted that she was sleeping around on him. So, William left Madison soon after.

Bruce Hand is the seven-year-old son of Madison Hand and William Jay.

Mandy Hand was single, never married and had no children (killed in Kringle, A Twisted Christmas Tale).

Robert Hand (died in Kringle, A Twisted Christmas Tale), brother of Morris hand.
    Robert married Natalie "Bond" Hand.
    Together, they had a son, Richard and two daughters, Brittany and Nancy.
    Robert had an affair with Dori Hand (see Morris Hand).

Natalie "Bond" Hand married Robert Hand (see Robert Hand).

Richard Hand married Dorothy "Brown" Hand.

Together, they have two daughters, Amy and Debra.
Richard had a drunken one-night stand with a woman named Marry who lives in the same trailer park as he does.

Dorothy "Brown" Hand married Richard Hand (see Richard Hand).

Amy and Debra Hand, daughters of Richard and Dorothy Hand.

Brittany "Hand" Anderson married Austin Anderson.
Together, they have three children, Julia, George and Ruby.
Brittany died in Kringle, Severed Bloodline, eight months pregnant with their fourth child.

Austin Anderson married Brittany hand (see Brittany "Hand" Anderson).

Julia, George and Ruby Anderson are children to Brittany and Austin Anderson.

Nancy "Hand" Long married Edward Long.
Together, they had four children, Diane, Kevin, Gary and Helen.

Edward Long married Nancy Hand (see Nancy "Hand" Long).

Diane, Kevin, Gary and Helen Long are the children of Nancy and Edward Long.

DELEATED SCENE #1

The following scene was going to be the original chapter for, "Whack-A-Mole" but then a much better idea came to mind so, instead of throwing out my original idea for the chapter, "Whack-A-Mole, here it is for you to read. You decide which version you like better.

WHACK-A-MOLE

Father Donovan is standing in the foyer of his house. He shuts and locks the front door and tosses his keys onto a stand that also has a telephone on it.

Father Donovan takes a deep breath then let's out a huge sigh.

As he starts to take off his coat, there's a knock on his front door.

Father Donovan hangs his coat on a hook then looks at his watch with a puzzled look. He's not expecting anyone at this hour. So, he wonders who it could be.

There's another knock.

As Father Donovan walks to his front door, "Who is it?" He asks.

There's no answer.

When Father Donovan reaches his door, he looks out the peephole. He sees a black woman standing at his door.

The woman is wearing a full length black gothic trench coat with a flared skirt.

The woman's hair is peppered with falling snow.

The woman steps away from the door, looks at the peephole and waves as if knowing she was being watched by someone. "Hi, my name is Twiggy. My car broke down a ways down the street. I was wondering if you had a phone, I could use to call for help."

There's a moment of silence then Father Donovan's door opens.

Father Donovan greets Twiggy with a smile. "Come in out of the cold weather, my deer." Father Donovan motions for Twiggy to come in.

Father Donovan then moves to the side to allow Twiggy to walk in.

Once Twiggy is in, Father Donovan pops his head out the door and quickly looks around. "And you said your car broke down?" Father Donovan sees no car.

Father Donovan steps back in his house and shuts his front door.

"Yes, down the street a little bit. I was on my way home to see my family. Twiggy smiles then, "Do you have a phone I can use to call someone to pick me up?" Twiggy asks.

"Sure, right there on the stand." Father Donovan points to a blue land line phone. "I was on my way to the kitchen to make some hot chocolate. Would you like some?" Father Donovan asks Twiggy.

"Sure, I'd love some." Twiggy responds with a smile.

"Alright then, I'll be right back with two cups of hot chocolate," Father Donovan turns and hurries into his kitchen to make the hot chocolate.

As Father Donovan prepares the hot chocolate, he hears Twiggy in the foyer talking to someone on the phone.

After a few minutes, Father Donovan doesn't hear anymore talking so he assumes the conversation has ended.

"So, did you find someone to come and look at your car?" Father Donovan asks Twiggy from in the kitchen as he finishes the hot chocolate.

Twiggy answers. "Oh yes, Father Donovan, my sisters are on their way."

Father Donovan has got a puzzled look on his face. He doesn't remember telling the woman his name.

Father Donovan picks the two cups of hot chocolate up. "If you don't mind me asking, how do you know my name?" Father Donovan heads to the foyer where he left Twiggy to make her phone call.

Twiggy answers Father Donovan's question. "Why Father Donovan, everyone up North knows who you are. You're the dirty priest who likes to raw doggin' in the fart box with little boys."

Just as Father Donovan is about to turn the corner and walk into the foyer, Twiggy's words stop him in his tracks. His eyes widen. Father Donovan's hands start to shake, spilling some of the hot chocolate.

Father Donovan decides, in the seconds that he is stopped in his tracks that it's best if he plays dumb.

Father Donovan takes a deep breath and calms down then, "Excuse me?" Father Donovan asks as he continues into the foyer.

When Father Donovan walks into the foyer with the hot chocolate, Twiggy is no longer there. Instead, in her place is a cute little, black tan rabbit that's sitting in the middle of the foyer.

The rabbit twitches its nose.

Father Donovan is surprised. He didn't expect to see a rabbit sitting in his foyer.

At first, Father Donovan is at lost for words then, "Twiggy?... Twiggy, are you here? I have your hot chocolate." Father Donovan calls out for Twiggy, but she still doesn't answer.

The rabbit twitches its nose again.

Father Donovan shrugs his shoulders then directs his attention to the rabbit sitting in front of him.

Father Donovan kneels down and sets the two cups of hot chocolate on the floor, beside him. He then reaches out for the rabbit.

"Oh, aren't you a cute little fella. Now how did you get in here?" Father Donovan inches closer to the rabbit.

As Father Donovan gets closer to the rabbit, the rabbit quickly jumps into the air and shapeshifts into Twiggy.

"I'm not a fella, you pedophile motherfucker!" In the blink of an eye, Twiggy lands a powerful snap kick to Father Donovan's chin, sending him flying backwards.

When Father Donovan lands, he hits the back of his head on the wooden floor, knocking him out.

Sometime later, Father Donovan is awakened by a big pot of ice-cold water thrown on his face by Cupid.

Father Donovan tries to sit up, gasping for air but he cannot. He's been quartered with his hands and feet tied to his couch and two chairs.

Father Donovan has also been stripped of his clothing from the waist down. His underwear has been stuffed into his mouth.

Twiggy walks into the same room as Father Donovan. She is holding a stainless-steel meat mallet that has rows of pyramid shaped tenderizers on either side of it.

"Time to wake up, Father Donovan." Twiggy tells Father Donovan as she hits the meat mallet on her hand a couple times.

Father Donovan shakes his head from side to side while blinking, trying to get the water out of his eyes so that he can see better.

Father Donovan has a look of horror on his face when he realizes the position he is in.

"Mother couldn't join us but, I did say my sisters would be here." Twiggy pauses for a moment, smiles then introduces her sisters, starting with Cupid. "The young lady who woke you out of your slumber is Genevieve, but everyone calls her Cupid."

Cupid smiles at Twiggy then curtsies.

Twiggy then introduces Pepper who is sitting in one of the chairs with her legs slung over an arm of the chair and sucking on a candy cane.

"That lady over there is Peppermint but all of her friends call her Pepper." Twiggy points to Pepper.

Father Donovan strains his head to try and get a look at the woman sucking on a candy cane.

Pepper doesn't say a word, she just nods her head while sucking on her candy cane.

Father Donovan mumbles as if he were trying to say something but is unable to because of his underwear stuffed in his mouth.

Twiggy puts a finger up to her mouth. "Shhh! Don't make this any harder than it is, you sick son-of-a-bitch." Twiggy stuffs Father Donovan's underwear further into his mouth. "And finally, the two ladies responsible for filling your house with such an intoxicating aroma, Vixen and Prancer." Twiggy looks at the couch where Vixen and Prancer are sitting, naked.

Prancer is sitting on Vixen's lap with her arms and legs wrapped around Vixen's back.

Vixen's hands are firmly gripping each one of Prancer's ass cheeks.

Prancer and Vixen have got their tongues down the other's throat. Both sisters moan as they suck longingly on each other's tongue.

Prancer arches her back as one of Vixen's hands slip deep into her sister's ass crack.

Everyone in the room watches intently as the twins make out on Father Donovan's couch.

Twiggy breaks the silence. "Oookay then." Twiggy

turns to a horror-stricken Father Donovan. "Now for the reason why we're here." Twiggy hits the meat mallet on her hand a few times. "It seems that you love to play corn hole with your altar boys." Twiggy pauses for a second then, "And that's something that cannot continue. So, we're here to put an end to that."

Father Donovan tries to scream through the gag in his mouth while thrashing around like a wild animal caught in a trap.

Pepper takes the candy cane out of her mouth and, "EEEW!" Pepper then turns to Cupid and asks, "What is corn hole?"

Cupid leans down and whispers in Pepper's ear while making a hand gesture towards her ass as if something were going in and out of it.

Pepper quickly looks at Father Donovan with a disgusted look on her face. She gives Father Donovan a light nudge with one of her feet. "Oooh! You sick crusty bastard." Pepper goes back to sucking on her cany cane.

As Twiggy kneels down between Father Donovan's legs, she sets the meat mallet and a roll of duct tape that she got off the couch, on the floor. Twiggy then grabs onto Father Donovan's legs to keep them from moving around. She can feel his legs trembling in her hands. "Oh, poor little guy. You're trembling. Is this how your altar boys felt moments before you plugged their ass?" Twiggy asks with a mischievous smile.

Cupid kneels down as well, just above Father Donovan's head. She holds his shoulders down.

Father Donovan quickly looks up at Cupid who is looking down at him.

"I suggest you calm yourself down and pray to your God and ask him for forgiveness because no one is going to hear you scream and there is no way in hell you're getting out of here alive." Twiggy tells Father Donovan.

Father Donovan is sweating profusely while struggling to breathe through his nose as he is still panic stricken.

"You know, I was going to kill you quick and end it there but, I thought about it and… fuck. You made a game out of fucking those poor little boys so, since you like to play games, we're going to play a game with you called, Whack-A-Mole." Twiggy looks at her sisters and, "Ladies, time to play."

By now, Prancer and Vixen have finished their little make out session and are now getting dressed.

Pepper puts what's left of her candy cane into her mouth then chews and swallows what's left in her mouth.

As the rest of Twiggy's sisters find a spot on the floor around Father Donovan, Twiggy picks up the duct tape. "First, before we start, we're going to have to move that little fucker out of the way." Twiggy refers to Father Donovan's small, limp penis.

All the women laugh and point at Father Donovan's small, limp penis.

Twiggy rips off a piece of duct tape and tapes Father's Donovan's penis to his inner thigh so that just his scrotum sack is exposed.

Father Donovan begins to cry hysterically. He even pisses himself.

"EEEW!" All the women say at the same time.

"You fucking pig." Twiggy says as she slams the meat mallet down onto Father Donovan's scrotum sack, smashing all of its contents.

Father Donovan screams as if his soul were being ripped from him by the Devil himself.

DELEATED SCENE #2

The following scene is from the chapter, Father Murphy's Twisted Confession.
I thought the scene was kind of boring and uneventful. To me, the scene needed more. So, I took out what I had originally wrote and rewrote it and added what I think was a little more toe curling excitement.
The following scene is what I originally wrote.
You can decide which version of the scene you like.

FATHER MURPHY'S TWISTED CONFESION

The grove of pine trees open up into a clearing and to Father Murphy's surprise, in the middle of the clearing is a Kondo Teak Platform Bed with bedsheets as white as the snow around it.

The bed is surrounded by holly and red poinsettias. There is also white fairy lights illuminating the whole bed.

But what really surprises Father Murphy is the pale, naked woman lying in the bed with her head at the foot of the bed.

Even though he is a man of God, Father Murphy's eyes still widen with excitement. He can't remember the last time he has seen the bare flesh of a woman. "Oh my." He whispers.

The naked woman doesn't seem to be bothered by the cold weather or the light fluffy snow that's still coming down.

Father Murphy's jaw really drops when he sees the reindeer approach the foot of the bed.

When the reindeer reaches the foot of the bed, it

slowly shapeshifts into another naked, pale woman who looks identical to the woman lying on the bed.

The woman slowly climbs up onto the foot of the bed and slowly lowers herself so she is face to face with the woman lying on the bed but in opposite directions.

Both women stick their tongues out, tantalizing each other. Then they stick their tongues deep into each other's mouth, sucking long and hard as if each other's tongues were sweet pieces of candy.

Father Murphy watches with both his mouth and eyes wide open. For fear that he might miss something, he doesn't dare blink.

The women stop their sucking on each other's tongues and slowly pull their tongues out of the other's mouth with a small string of spit connecting their tongues.

The women turn to Father Murphy and smile. With their index finger they both motion for Father Murphy to join them.

Just as Father Murphy takes a step towards the women on the bed, he hears a woman whispering in his ear again. "Nicolas Murphy."

My Oscar Speech

Since publishing my first book as an indie author on June 14th, 2015, I've had lots of help over the years, getting me to where I am as an author, whether it was the encouraging words from friends near and far to keep me going, advice on what I should or shouldn't do or my beta readers. Hell, even the negativity I got on some of my characters in the first Kringle helped make me who I am today.

I'm 100% positive, the worlds that I have created wouldn't be possible without all of you.

So, as a way to show my appreciation for all of your help, I would like to mention all those who had a hand in making this world that I've created possible.

Normally, someone would call this section the acknowledgements but, I'm going to call it, My Oscar Speech. Why? Because when someone gives an acceptance speech for their Oscar, the speech seems to go on forever and ever and ever and ever. And that is what this section does, I have a lot of people to mention, and it goes on and on and on.

So, here I go.

My Beta readers for Kringle, Severed Bloodline: **Sibbie**, **Tabatha** and **Heidi**. Thank you.

The cover model who offered her eyes for the cover, **Tabitha**.

The out of this world cover artist with an amazing talent, **Ryan**. You and your talents rock.

To those who volunteered to be on Santa's naughty or nice

list, thank you: **Becky, Theresa, Tabatha, Rex, Jenna** and **Nicky**.

Holly's cloak design for the chapter, "Coach Stall's Emasculation": **Justin, Wendi** and **Linda**.

For those who helped with the last name for Holly's father: **Katia, Brice, Lucas** and **Frank**.

A big thank you goes out to **Theresa** for inspiring a conversation between Holly and Gammy that had to do with being perfectly imperfect.

When it came time to decide between leather bondage or Japanese rope bondage, these following people had a say as to what was used: **Ripley, Jerry, Iris, Sibbie, Carrie, Frank, Husen, Nathan, Helen, Edith, Tammy, Paulie, Michelle, Carrie, Shelley** and **Tanmay**.

The list of offensive Christmas songs was provided by **Wendi** and **Edith**.

Holly's bathtub design, **Michelle**.

In the chapter, "It's All About The Win" the play-by-play announcement was provided by **Marty**.

Character development consultants, **Wendi** (Cupid's measurements) and **Heidi** (Twiggy's measurements).

The size of Cupid's bow and other useful information on archery was provided by my archer friend from across the pond, **Nicky**.

When it came time to dress Cupid, these following people

had an opinion: **Shelly, Siddie, Wendi, Pam, Mary, Natalie, Kya, Genneke** and **Carrie.**

Cupid's hairstyle was provided by: **Carrie, Brice, Kya, Ann Ripley, Sibbie** and **Serina.**

Holly and Cupid's hair design got a big help from **Heidi** and **Victoria.**

When it came time to design Holly's bathroom, these following people were a big help: **Kya, Michael** and **Nikki.**

The candle lantern in Kringle, Severed Bloodline was inspired and designed by the talented **Cyndi.**

My Mission Statement

When I first started writing horror, my goal was not to be another Bram Stoker, Stephen King, Dean Koontz or Clive Barker. Oh sure, they are some of the best writers the horror world has to offer but I mean really, where is the fun in following in the footsteps of someone who has already achieved greatness?

My goal when I first started to write and as I continue to write now, is to step outside the box and dare to be different from all the rest.

I write stories that I think should be written and write them my way.

The thought behind my stories is to leave my readers shocked and surprised. I want to leave my readers saying… "WHAT THE FUCK!"

If you liked reading Kringle, Severed Bloodline and would like to read more of my twisted and disturbing stories, please go to my Amazon author page.

https://www.amazon.com/Ron-Chapman/e/B00PZBDEUW

Or you can stalk me at any of my social media sites and read all about my book projects, book releases or any other writing related news about my twisted and disturbed world.

Instagram:
www.instagram.com/ronchapman69 or @Ronchapman69

Twitter:
www.twitter.com/ronmtdew or @RonMtDew

Pinterest:
www.pinterest.com/ronchapman69

Facebook:
http://facebook.com/Ronchapman69

And then there's **Vero**, the only **True Social** media site. It is here where you'll get exclusive information before anyone else, on my books or any other twisted and disturbing shit that I may write.

Vero:
vero.co/ronchapman

You will not be disappointed, I promise.

Made in the USA
Middletown, DE
18 November 2023